Edward Sylvester Ellis

Klondike Nuggets

And How Two Boys Secured them

Edward Sylvester Ellis

Klondike Nuggets
And How Two Boys Secured them

ISBN/EAN: 9783337275082

Printed in Europe, USA, Canada, Australia, Japan

Cover: Foto ©Andreas Hilbeck / pixelio.de

More available books at **www.hansebooks.com**

THE HEAD AND SHOULDERS OF A MAN INTENTLY STUDYING
THEM

KLONDIKE NUGGETS

AND

HOW TWO BOYS SECURED THEM

BY

E. S. ELLIS

AUTHOR OF
" Deerfoot Series," " Boy-Pioneer Series," etc.

24 ILLUSTRATIONS AFTER
ORSON LOWELL

DOUBLEDAY & McCLURE CO.
NEW YORK
1898

CONTENTS

LIST OF ILLUSTRATIONS.

LIST OF ILLUSTRATIONS.

KLONDIKE NUGGETS

AND

HOW TWO BOYS SECURED THEM

KLONDIKE NUGGETS AND

HOW TWO BOYS SECURED THEM.

CHAPTER I.

THE GOLD-HUNTERS.

JEFF GRAHAM was an Argonaut who crossed the plains in 1849, while he was yet in his teens, and settling in California, made it his permanent home. When he left Independence, Mo., with the train, his parents and one sister were his companions, but all of them were buried on the prairie, and their loss robbed him of the desire ever to return to the East. Hostile Indians, storm, cold, heat, privation, and suffering were the causes of their taking off, as they have been of hundreds who undertook the long journey to the Pacific coast in quest of gold.

Jeff spent several years in the diggings, and after varying fortune, made a strike, which yielded him sufficient to make him comfortable for the rest of his days. He never married, and the income from his investments was all and, indeed, more than he needed to secure him against want.

He was now past threescore, grizzled, somewhat stoop-shouldered, but robust, rugged, strong, and, in his way, happy. His dress varied slightly with the changes of the seasons, consisting of an old slouch hat, a red shirt, coarse trousers tucked in the tops of his heavy boots, and a black neckerchief with dangling ends. He had never been addicted to drink, and his only indulgence was his brierwood pipe, which was his almost inseparable companion. His trousers were secured at the waist by a strong leathern belt, and when he wore a coat in cold weather he generally had a revolver at his hip, but the weapon had not been discharged in years.

There were two members of that overland train whom Jeff never forgot. They were young children, Roswell and Edith Palmer, who lost both of their parents within five years after reaching the coast. Jeff proved the friend in need, and no father could have been kinder to the orphans, who were ten and twelve years younger than he.

Roswell Palmer was now married, with a son named for himself, while his sister, Mrs. Mansley, had been a widow a long time, and she, too, had an only son, Frank, who was a few months older than his cousin. The boys had received a good common-school education, but their parents were too poor to send them to college. Jeff would have offered to help but for his prejudice against all colleges. The small wages which the lads received as clerks in a leading dry-goods house were needed by their parents, and the youths, active, lusty, and ambitious, had settled down to the career of merchants, with the hoped-for reward a long, long way in the future.

One evening late in March, 1897, Jeff opened the door of Mr. Palmer's modest home, near the northern suburb of San Francisco, and with his pipe between his lips, sat down in the chair to which he was always welcome. In truth, the chair was considered his, and no one would have thought of occupying it when he was present. As he slowly puffed his pipe he swayed gently backward and forward, his slouch hat on the floor beside him, and his long, straggling hair dangling about his shoulders, while his heavy beard came almost to his eyes.

It was so late that the wife had long since cleared away the dishes from the table, and sat at one side of the room sewing by the lamp. The husband was reading a paper, but laid it aside when Jeff entered, always glad to talk with their quaint visitor, to whom he and his family were bound by warm ties of gratitude.

Jeff smoked a minute or two in silence, after greeting his friends, and the humping of his massive shoulders showed that he was laughing, though he gave forth no sound.

" What pleases you, Jeff ?" asked Mr. Palmer, smiling in sympathy, while the wife looked at their caller in mild surprise.

" I've heerd it said that a burned child dreads the fire, but I don't b'lieve it. After he's burnt he goes back agin and gits burnt over. Why is it, after them explorers that are trying to find the North Pole no sooner git home and thawed out than they're crazy to go back agin ? Look at Peary. You'd think he had enough, but he's at it once more, and will keep at it after he finds the pole—that is, if he ever does find it. Nansen, too, he'll be like a fish out of water till he's climbing the icebergs agin.''

And once more the huge shoulders bobbed up and down. His friends knew this was meant to serve as an introduction to something else that was on Jeff's mind, and they smilingly waited for it to come.

'' It's over forty years since I roughed it in the diggings, starving, fighting Injins, and getting tough,'' continued the old miner musingly. '' After I struck it purty fair I quit ; but I never told you how many times the longing has come over me so strong that it was all I could do to stick at home and not make a fool of myself.''

'' But that was in your younger days,'' replied his friend ; '' you have had nothing of the kind for a good while.''

Jeff took his pipe from the network of beard that enclosed his lips, and turned his bright, gray eyes upon the husband and wife who were looking curiously at him. They knew by the movement of the beard at the corners of the invisible mouth that he was smiling.

"There's the joke. It's come over me so strong inside the last week, that I've made up my mind to start out on a hunt for gold. What do you think of that, eh?"

And restoring his pipe to his lips, he leaned back and rocked his chair with more vigor than before, while he looked fixedly into the faces of his friends.

"Jeff, you can't be in earnest; you are past threescore—"

"Sixty-four last month," he interrupted; "let's git it right."

"And you are in no need of money; besides it is a hard matter to find any place in California where it is worth your while—"

"But it ain't Californy," he broke in again; "it's the Klondike country. No use of talking," he added with warmth, "there's richer deposits in Alaska and that part of the world than was ever found hereabouts. I've got a friend, Tim McCabe, at Juneau; he's been through the Klondike country, and writes me there's no mistake about it; he wants me to join him. I'm going to do it, and your boy Roswell and his cousin Frank are to go with me. Oh, it's all settled," said Jeff airily;

JEFF.

"the only question is how soon you can git him ready. A day oughter be enough."

The husband and wife looked at each other in astonishment. They had not dreamed of anything like this; but if the truth were told, Mr. Palmer had been so wrought up by the wonderful stories that were continually coming from Alaska and British Columbia, that he was seriously thinking of joining the northward-bound procession.

Startling as was the announcement of Jeff Graham, a discussion of the scheme brought out more than one fact to recommend it. The youths were in perfect health, strong and athletic. Jeff volunteered to provide all the funds needed, and his early experience in mining and his love for the boys made him an invaluable guide and companion despite his years. He had turned over in his mind every phase of the question, and met each objection the affectionate mother brought forward, alarmed as she was at the thought of having her boy go so many miles from under her care.

"It will be necessary to talk with Roswell about it," said the father, after the conversation had lasted a considerable while.

"No, it won't; I've talked with him, and he's as crazy as me to go."

"But what will Frank's mother say?"

"She's said what she's got to say; had a talk with her last night, and it's all fixed.   I've sent word to Tim that I'll be at Juneau by next steamer, and have two of the likeliest younkers with me on the coast; then we'll head for the Upper Yukon, and bime-by hire a ship to bring back all the gold we'll scoop in."

"It seems to me that we have nothing to do in the premises, Jeff."

"Nothing 'cept to git the youngster ready."

CHAPTER II.

Now it is a serious undertaking for any one to make a journey to the gold regions at the headwaters of the Yukon, as every one will admit who has been there. All know of the starvation which threatened the people of Dawson City during the winter of 1897–98, when the whole country was stirred with sympathy, and our Government made use of reindeer to take food to the suffering miners.

No dangers of that kind confronted Roswell Palmer and Frank Mansley, but their parents could not contemplate the undertaking without anxiety. The mothers held more than one consultation, and there was a time when both were inclined to object to the boys going at all. The dread of that desolate, icy region in the far Northwest grew upon them, until it is safe to say that if the departure had been postponed for only a few days Mrs. Mansley and Mrs. Palmer would never have given their consent. But Mr. Palmer laughed at their fears, and assured them there was no cause for alarm. He spoke so cheeringly that they caught his hopefulness, but neither noticed the lump he swallowed, nor with what difficulty he kept back the tears when the hour for parting came. He was fully as anxious as they, but he knew how to dissemble, and would not have confessed his real emotions for the world.

After all, it was Jeff Graham who deserved the credit for the willingness of the parents to see their sons venture upon the long and dangerous journey. To him the trip was much the same as a visit to Los Angeles or the Yosemite Valley. His self-confidence never faltered. He was sure it would be only a pleasant outing, with the certainty of a big reward at the end of it. The sly fellow dwelt on the pale complexion and debilitated appearance of the lads. He even said that a cough which he heard Frank try to suppress (in swallowing some fruit, a bit of it went the " wrong way"—it was nothing more) indicated the insidious approach of consumption. Jeff was the only one who was able to see any paleness in the countenance of the young athletes, or suspect them of being otherwise than fine specimens of youthful health and vigor; but since he was as solemn as a judge when making his declaration, the father and mother of the one and the mother of the other could not feel quite certain there were not grounds for his fears.

And so it being settled that the boys were to go to the Klondike gold fields under the care of the grim old Argonaut, it only remained to complete the preparations in the short time at their disposal.

Had the mothers been free to carry out their wishes, their sons would have been loaded down with baggage upon leaving San Francisco. There are so many things which seem indispensable, when an affectionate mother is considering the comfort of her only son, that she is sure to overwhelm him. At first the mothers insisted upon each being furnished with a large trunk, which would have to be crowded to bursting to contain what was needed, but Jeff put his foot down.

"Nothin' of the kind. Didn't I tell you that we'll git all that's needed at Juneau or

Dyea or some point on the road ?   You've forgot that."

" But, Jeff, there are some articles which
they *must* take with them."

The old miner lit his pipe, sat down in the
rocking-chair at the Palmer home, where the
mothers had met while the boys and Mr. Palmer were down-town making a few forgotten
purchases.   The old fellow chuckled a little and
then became serious.

" In the fust place, not a trunk !" and he
shook his head decisively.

" Do you expect them to take what they
want in their pockets ?"

" Umph ! it would be the sensiblest thing
they could do, but we can't be bothered with
any trunks, that would be sure to be lost in the
first shuffle.   Each of us will have a good, big,
strong carpet-bag, and nothing more.   You can
cram them as full as you choose, but what you
can't git in has got to be left at home."

There could be no mistake as to Jeff's earnestness, and neither mother attempted to gainsay
his words.

" Now," said he, " jest lay out on the floor
what you have in your mind that the young-

sters need, and I'll tell you what they *do* need."

"You mustn't forget," observed Mrs. Palmer, as she started to comply, "that the boys are now down-town buying some things which they positively cannot get along without."

"As, for instance, what?"

"Well, tooth-brushes, soap, combs, court-plaster, handkerchiefs, buttons, thread, quinine, and pain-killer."

"Is that all?" asked Jeff so quizzically that both ladies laughed.

"You have forgotten," added Mrs. Mansley, "the shirts, underclothing, socks, and shoes."

"They are here," replied Mrs. Palmer, stepping briskly into the next room and returning with her arms full.

"I've got to lay down the law," observed Jeff, just as Mr. Palmer and the two boys came in, glowing with excitement. "Here are the young men, and they look as if they had bought out half the town. Dump everything on the floor, and let's sort 'em out."

When the pile was complete the miner gravely remarked:

"Nothing less than a freight-car will answer

for all that stuff, and I don't b'lieve we can
charter one through to Dawson.   In the first
place, I s'pose the tooth-brushes will have to go,
though I never found any use for such things,
and I can crack a bull hickory-nut with my
teeth.   The same may be observed of the soap
and combs, while a roll of court plaster don't
take up much room.   We'll be likely to need
thread, buttons, and some patches for our
clothes, though I've got a supply in my carpet-
bag.   The quinine and pain-killer they may
take if you can find a corner to squeeze 'em
in.   As to the underclothing, extra shirts, it
depends whether there is room for 'em; but the
boys mustn't think of taking their dress suits
along, 'cause *I'm* not going to.   There ain't
any room for violins, pianos, or music-boxes,
and the only clothing and shoes that can go
with this party is what we wear on our bodies
and feet."

"Suppose the shoes wear out?" asked Mrs.
Mansley in dismay.

"Then we'll go barefoot.   Now, see here,
we shan't be away more than three months.
A pair of well-made shoes will last longer than
that, and the same is true about our clothes.

though we have the means of mending them, if modesty calls for it, which ain't likely to be the case in the diggings. Caps, coats, vests, trousers, and shoes are to sarve from the day we start till we come back. If one of the boys casts a shoe and loses it, we'll find some way of getting him another. What's this?" suddenly asked Jeff, picking up a small volume from the floor and opening it.

He looked at the fly-leaf, on which was written : "To my dear boy Roswell, from his affectionate mother. Read a portion every day, and be guided in your thoughts, words, and deeds by its blessed precepts. Then it shall always be well with thee."

There were two of the small Bibles, the other being similarly inscribed with the name of Frank Mansley. The boys and their parents were standing around the seated miner, and no one spoke. He looked at each precious volume in turn, and then reverently laid them among the pile of indispensables.

"That's the mother of it," he said, as if speaking with himself; "it's a good many years since my poor old mother done the same thing for me when I started for Californy, and

I've got the book among my things yet, though I don't read it as often as I should. *Them* go if we have to leave everything else behind.''

When the task was completed, every one acknowledged the excellent judgment displayed by Jeff Graham. The three were arrayed in strong, thick, warm clothing, and, in addition, each carried a heavy overcoat on his arm. In the valises were crowded underclothing, shirts, handkerchiefs, and the articles that have been already specified. It was wonderful how skilfully the mothers did the packing. When it looked as if every inch of space was filled, they found a crevice into which another bottle of standard medicine, an extra bit of soap, more thread and needles and conveniences of which no other person would think were forced without adding to the difficulty of locking the valises.

Nothing remaining to be done, on the following day the boys kissed their tearful mothers good-by, and warmly shook hands with Mr. Palmer, who brokenly murmured, '' God bless you ! be good boys !'' as he saw them off on the steamer bound for Seattle, and thence to Juneau, where they safely arrived one day early in April, 1897.

In making such a voyage, many people are necessarily thrown together in more or less close companionship, with the result of forming numerous acquaintances and sometimes lasting friendships. Following the advice of Jeff, the cousins had little to say about their plans, though they became interested in more than one passenger, and often speculated between themselves as to the likelihood of certain ones meeting success or failure in the gold regions.

There were three sturdy lumbermen all the way from Maine. A curious fact about them was that, although they were not related at all, the name of each was Brown. They were light-hearted and the life of the large party. One Brown had a good tenor voice, and often sang popular ballads with taste and great acceptability. Another played the violin with considerable skill, and sometimes indulged in jig tunes, to which his friends, and occasionally others, danced an accompaniment.

" They'll succeed," was the verdict of Roswell, " for they are strong, healthy, and will toil like beavers."

"And what of the two men smoking their pipes just beyond the fiddler?" asked Frank.

"I had a talk with them the other day; one has been a miner in Australia, and the other spent two years in the diamond mines of Kimberley, South Africa. Meeting for the first time in San Francisco, they formed a partnership; they, too, are rugged and must understand their business."

"No doubt of it. Do you remember that stoop-shouldered old man whose room is next to ours?"

"The one who has such dreadful coughing spells in the night?"

"Yes; he is far gone with consumption, and yet he won't believe there's anything the matter with him. He is worse than when he came on board; but he says it is only a slight cold which will soon pass off, and he is just as hopeful as you or I of taking a lot of nuggets home with him."

"He never will see the other side of Chilkoot Pass."

"I doubt whether he will ever see this side."

Thus the boys speculated, sometimes amused and sometimes saddened by what they saw.

There was a big San Francisco policeman, who said he had cracked heads so long that he thought he knew how to crack some golden nuggets ; a correspondent of a prominent New York newspaper, whose situation was enviable, since his salary and expenses were guaranteed, and he was free to gather gold when the opportunity offered ; a voluble insurance agent, who made a nuisance of himself by his solicitations, in season and out ; a massive football-player, who had no companion, and did not wish any, since he was sure he could buck the line, make a touchdown, and kick a goal ; a gray-haired head of a family, who, having lost his all, had set out to gather another fortune along the Klondike. He walked briskly, threw back his shoulders, and tried hard to appear young and vigorous, but the chances were strongly against him. There were a number of bright clerks; a clergyman, pleasant and genial with all ; gamblers, with pallid faces and hair and mustaches dyed an intense black, who expected to win the gold for which others dug ; young and middle-aged men, some with their brave wives, serene and calmly prepared to bear their full share of privation and toil ; and adventurers, ready to go anywhere for the sake of adventure itself. In truth, it was a motley assemblage, which to the boys was like a continually shifting panorama of hope, ambition, honesty, dishonor, pluck, and human enterprise and daring, that was ever present throughout the thousand miles of salt water that stretches from Seattle to Juneau.

Juneau, the metropolis of Alaska, was founded in 1880, and named in honor of Joseph Juneau, the discoverer of gold on Douglas Island, two miles distant. There is located the Treadwell quartz-mill, the largest in the world. The city nestles at the base of a precipitous mountain, thirty-three hundred feet high, has several thousand inhabitants, with its wooden houses regularly laid out, good wharves, water works, electric lights, banks, hotels, newspapers, schools, and churches.

" Here's where we get our outfit," said Jeff, as they hurried over the plank to the landing. " But where can Tim be ?"

He paused abruptly as soon as he was clear of the crowd, and looked around for the one who was the cause of his coming to this out-of-the-way corner of the world. He was still gazing when a man, dressed much the same as himself, but short, stockily built, and with the reddest hair and whiskers the boys had ever seen, his round face aglow with pleasure stepped hastily forward from the group of spectators and extended his hand.

" Ah, Jiff, it does me good to see your handsome silf ; and how have ye been, and how do ye expect to continue to be ?"

Tim McCabe was an Irishman who, when overtaken by misfortune in San Francisco, found Jeff Graham the good Samaritan, and he could never show sufficient gratitude therefor. It was only one of the many kindly deeds the old miner was always performing, but he did not meet in every case with such honest thankfulness.

Jeff clasped his hand warmly, and then looked at the smiling boys, to whom he introduced his friend, and who shook their hands. He eyed them closely, and, with the quizzical expression natural to many of his people, said :

" And these are the laddies ye wrote me about ? Ye said they were likely broths of boys; but, Jiff, ye didn't do them justice—they desarved more."

" Tim is always full of blarney," explained Jeff, who, it was evident, was fond of the merry Irishman ; " so you mustn't mind him and his ways."

Roswell and Frank were attracted by Jeff's friend. He was one of those persons who, despite their homeliness of face and feature, win us by their genial nature and honest, outspoken ways. No one ever saw a finer set of big, white teeth, nor a broader smile, which scarcely ever was absent from the Irishman's countenance. He shook hands with each lad in turn, giving a warm pressure and expressing his pleasure at meeting them. " I'm glad to greet ye, me friends," he said, as the whole party moved out of the way of the hurrying, bustling swarm who were rushing back and forth, each intent on his own business ; " not only on your own account, but on account of me friend Jiff."

" I do not quite understand you," said Roswell with a smile.

" Well, you see, I've met Jiff before, and formed a rather fair opinion of him ; but whin a gintleman like mesilf is engaged on some important business, them as are to be favored

with me confidence must have their creden-
tials."

"And you accept our presence with him as
proof that he is what he should be ?"

Tim gravely inclined his head.

"Do ye think I would admit Jiff as a partner if it was otherwise ? Not I."

"But," interposed Frank, "how is it with
us ? You never saw us before."

"One look at them faces is enough," was
the prompt reply ; "ye carry a certificate wid
ye that no one can dispoot."

"And I should like to know," said Jeff,
with assumed indignation, "what credential
you have to present to us, young man."

"Mine is the same as the young gintlemen,"
answered Tim, removing his thick fur cap and
displaying his whole wealth of fiery red hair ;
"obsarve me countenance."

His face became grave for the first time,
while all the rest laughed.

"I'm satisfied and hungry," said Jeff ;
"take us where we can get something to eat."

"I knew by that token that I had forgot
something, and it's me breakfast and dinner.
In honor of yer coming, I've engaged the

best quarters at the leading hotel.   Come wid
me."

It was but a short distance up the street to a
frame hotel, which was kept by a corpulent
German who had been in the country for a
couple of years.   The men registered, during
which Tim remarked to the landlord, who
seemed never to be without his long-stemmed
meerschaum pipe between his lips :

" This gintleman isn't the burglar that ye
would think from his looks.   He belongs to a
good family, or ye wouldn't obsarve him in my
company.   The young gintlemen are two
princes that are travelling *in cog.*   In consideration of all of them having delicate appetites
like mesilf, not forgetting the honor of their
company, ye will be glad to make a reduction
in your exorbitant rates, Baron Fritz, I am
sure."

The phlegmatic German smiled, and in a
guttural voice announced that his terms were
three dollars a day, including rooms and meals,
which, when all the circumstances are considered, was not extravagant.   The party carried
their luggage to their rooms, where they prepared themselves for the meal, which was satis-

factory in every respect and better than they expected.

It came out during the conversation that Tim McCabe had not a dollar to his name, and he spoke the truth when he said that he had not eaten a mouthful that day. It would have gone hard for him but for the arrival of Jeff Graham, though there is such a lively demand for labor in Juneau that he must have soon found means to provide himself with food.

As for Jeff, he was glad in his heart that his old friend was in such sore straits, inasmuch as it gave him the pleasure of providing for him. Tim had taken out some five hundred dollars, but a companion whom he fully trusted robbed him of it, and the small amount left barely kept the Irishman afloat until the arrival of the old miner.

Jeff Graham showed prudence in bringing a plentiful supply of funds with him, and since he expected to take back a hundredfold more than he brought, he could well afford to do so. Stowed away in his safe inside pocket was fully two thousand dollars, and inasmuch as gold is the " coin of the realm" in California, as well as in Alaska, the funds were in shining eagles and half eagles—rather bulky of themselves, but not uncomfortably so.

The experience of McCabe and Jeff prevented any mistake in providing their outfit. They had good, warm flannels, thick woollen garments, strong shoes, and rubber boots. Those who press their mining operations during the long and severe winter generally use the water boot of seal and walrus, which costs from two dollars to five dollars a pair, with trousers made from Siberian fawn-skins and the skin of the marmot and ground squirrel, with the outer garment of marmot-skin. Blankets and robes, of course, are indispensable. The best are of wolf-skin, and Jeff paid one hundred dollars apiece for those furnished to himself and each of his companions.

The matter of provisions was of the first importance. A man needs a goodly supply of nourishing food to sustain him through the trying journey from Juneau to Dawson City, the following being considered necessary for an able-bodied person : Twenty pounds of flour, twelve of bacon, twelve of beans, four of butter, five of vegetables, five of sugar, three of coffee, five of corn-meal, one pound of tea, four cans of condensed milk, one and one half pounds of salt, with a little pepper and mustard.

Because of the weight and bulk, Jeff omitted from this list the tea, the condensed milk and butter, and while the supply in other respects was the same, respectively, for himself and McCabe, that of the boys was cut down about one third; for besides the food, the party were compelled to take with them a frying-pan, a water-kettle, a Yukon stove, a bean-pot, a drinking-cup, knives and forks, and a large and small frying-pan.

Since they would find a good raft necessary, axes, hatchets, hunting-knives, nails, one hundred and fifty feet of rope, and two Juneau sleds were purchased. To these were added snow-shoes, a strong duck-tent, fishing-tackle, snow-glasses to protect themselves against snow-blindness, rubber blankets, mosquito-netting, tobacco, and a few minor articles.

The start from Juneau to the gold fields should not be made before the beginning of April. Our friends had struck that date, but the headlong rush did not begin until some time later. One of the principal routes is from Seattle to St. Michael, on the western coast of Alaska, and then up that mighty river whose mouth is near, for nearly two thousand more miles to Dawson City. The river is open during the summer—sometimes barely four months—and our friends took the shorter route to Juneau on the southern coast, from which it is about a thousand miles to Dawson. While this route is much shorter, it is a hundred times more difficult and dangerous than by the Yukon.

From Juneau there are four different routes to the headwaters of the Yukon, all crossing by separate paths the range of mountains along the coast. They are the Dyea or Chilkoot Pass, the Chilkat, Moore's or White Pass, and Takou. At this writing the Chilkoot is the favorite, because it is better known than the others, but the facilities for passing through this entrance or doorway to the new El Dorado are certain to be greatly increased at an early day.

It was learned on inquiry that another day would have to be spent in the town before the little steamer would leave for Dyea. While Tim and Jeff stayed at the hotel, talking over old times and laying plans for the future, the boys strolled through the streets, which were knee-deep with mud.

"ROSWELL, DO YOU KNOW THAT STRANGE MAN HAS BEEN
FOLLOWING US FOR THE PAST HOUR?"

The curio shops on Front and Seward streets were interesting, and from the upper end of the latter street they saw a path leading to the Auk village, whose people claim to own the flats at the mouth of Gold Creek. On the high ground across the stream is a cemetery containing a number of curious totemic carvings, hung with offerings to departed spirits. It would cost a white man his life to disturb any of them.

It was early in the afternoon that the cousins were strolling aimlessly about and had turned to retrace their steps to the hotel, when Frank touched the arm of his companion and said, in a low voice :

" Roswell, do you know that a strange man has been following us for the past hour ?"

" No ; where is he ?"

" On the other side of the street and a little way behind us. Don't look around just now. I don't fancy his appearance."

A minute later, Roswell managed to gain a good view.

" I don't like his looks as well as he seems to like ours. Shall we wait for him and ask him his business ?"

" No need of that, for he is walking so fast, he will soon be up with us. Here he comes, as if in a great hurry."

A few minutes later the boys were overtaken by the suspicious stranger.

CHAPTER III.

ROSWELL and Frank were standing in front of one of the curio stores, studying the interesting exhibits, among which was a pan of Klondike gold, but they kept watch of the stranger, who slouched up to them and halted at the side of Frank.

" I say, pards," he said in the gruff, wheedling tones of the professional tramp, " can't you do something for a chap that's down on his luck ?"

As the lads turned to face him they saw an unclean, tousled man, very tall, with stooping shoulders, protruding black eyes, spiky hair, and a generally repellent appearance.

" What's the trouble ?" asked Frank, looking into the face that had not been shaven for several days.

" Had the worst sort of luck ; got back from Klondike two days ago with thirty thousand dollars, and robbed of every cent. I'm dead broke."

"You seem to have had enough to buy whiskey," remarked Roswell, who had had a whiff of his breath, and placed no faith in his story. The man looked angrily at them, but restrained himself, in hopes of receiving help.

"There's where you're mistaken, my friends; I haven't had anything to eat for two days, and when a stranger offered me a swallow of whiskey to keep up my strength, I took it, as a medicine. If it hadn't been for that, I'd have flunked right in the street—sure as you live. What are you doing, if I may ask, in Juneau?"

"We are listening to you just now, but we are on our way to the gold fields," replied Roswell.

"Not alone?"

"We are going with two men, one of whom has been there before."

"That's more sensible. Let me give you a little advice—"

"We really do not feel the need of it," interposed Roswell, who liked the man less each minute. "You must excuse us, as we wish to join them at the hotel. Good-day."

"See here," said the fellow angrily, as he laid his hand on the arm of Frank; "ain't you going to stake me a bit?"

The lad shook off his grasp.

"Even if we wished to do so, we could not, for our friend at the hotel has all the funds that belong to our party. Perhaps if you go there, and he believes the story, Mr. Graham may do something for you, but Tim McCabe has not the means with which to help anybody."

At mention of the Irishman's name the fellow showed some agitation. Then, seeing that he was about to lose the expected aid, he uttered a savage expression and exclaimed:

"I don't believe a word you say."

"It is no concern of ours whether you believe it or not," replied Roswell, as he and Frank started down the street toward their hotel. The fellow was amazed at the defiance of the lads, and stood staring at them and muttering angrily to himself. Could he have carried out his promptings, he would have robbed both, but was restrained by several reasons.

In the first place, Juneau, despite the influx

of miners, is a law-abiding city, and the man's arrest and punishment would have followed speedily. Moreover, it would not have been an altogether "sure thing" for him to attack the youths. They were exceptionally tall, active and strong, and would have given him trouble without appeal to the firearms which they carried.

They looked round and smiled, but he did not follow them. When they reached the hotel they related the incident.

" Would ye oblige me with a description of the spalpeen ?" said Tim McCabe, after they had finished. Roswell did as requested.

" Be the powers, it's him !" exclaimed Tim. "I 'spected it when ye told the yarn which I've heerd he has been telling round town."

" Whom do you mean ?" asked Frank.

" Hardman, Ike Hardman himsilf."

" Who is he ?"

" Didn't I tell ye he was the one that robbed me of my money ? Sure I did, what is the matter wid ye ?"

" You told us about being robbed," said Jeff, " but didn't mention the name of the man who did it."

" I want to inthrodooce mesilf to him !" exclaimed Tim, flushed with indignation; " axscoose me for a bit."

He strode to the door with the intention of hunting up and chastising the rogue, but, with his hand on the knob, checked himself. For a moment he debated with himself, and then, as his broad face lit up with his natural good humor, he came back to his chair, paraphrasing Uncle Toby :

" The world's big enough for the likes of him and me, though he does crowd a bit. Let him git all the good out of the theft he can, say I."

Dyea is at the head of navigation, and is the timber line, being a hundred miles to the northwest of Juneau. It is at the upper fork of what is termed Lynn Canal, the most extensive fiord on the coast. It is, in truth, a continuation of Chatham Strait, the north and south passage being several hundred miles in extent, the whole forming the trough of a glacier which disappeared ages ago.

On the day following the incident described our friends boarded the little, untidy steam launch bound for Dyea. There were fifty pas-

sengers beside themselves, double the number
it was intended to carry, the destination of all
being the gold fields. The weather was keen
and biting, and the accommodations on the
boat poor. They pushed here and there, sur-
veying with natural interest the bleak scenery
along shore, the mountains white with snow,
and foretelling the more terrible regions that
lay beyond. Hundreds of miles remained to
be traversed before they could expect to gather
the yellow particles, but neither of the sturdy
lads felt any abatement of courage.

"Well, look at that!" suddenly exclaimed
Roswell, catching the arm of his companion
as they were making their way toward the
front of the boat.

Frank turned in the direction indicated, and
his astonishment was as great as his companion's. Tim McCabe and the shabby scamp,
Ike Hardman, were sitting near each other on
a bench, and smoking their pipes like two affectionate brothers. No one would have suspected
there had ever been a ripple between them.

Catching the eye of the amazed boys, Tim
winked and threw up his chin as an invitation
for them to approach. Frank shook his head,

CATCHING THE EYE OF THE AMAZED BOYS, TIM WINKED.

and he and Roswell went back to where Jeff was smoking his pipe. They had hardly time to tell their story when the Irishman joined them.

" I obsarved by the exprission on your faces that ye were a bit surprised," he said, addressing the youths.

" Is that fellow the Hardman you told us about ?" asked Roswell.

" The same at your sarvice."

" And the man who robbed you of your money ?"

Tim flung one of his muscular legs over the other, and with a twinkle of the eyes said :

" Hardman has made it all right ; the matter is fixed atween oursilves."

" Then he give you back your money ?" was the inquiring remark of Jeff.

" Not precisely that, though he said he would do the same if he only had it with him, but he run up agin a game at Juneau and was cleaned out. Whin he told me that I was a bit sorry for him. He further obsarved that it was his intintion if he won to stake me agin and add something extra for interest on what he borrowed of me. That spakes well for Hardman, so we shook hands over it," was the hearty conclusion of Tim.

The boys were too astonished to speak. Jeff Graham's shoulders shook, and he looked sideways at his friend with a quizzical expression, unable to do justice to his feelings. As for Tim, his red face was the picture of bland innocence, but he was not through. Astounding as were the statements he had just made, he had a still more astounding one to submit.

CHAPTER IV.

THE AVALANCHE.

It was late in the day that the little steamer arrived at Dyea, which was found to be a village with one log store, a number of movable tents, and without any wharf, the beach being so flat that at high water the tide reaches a half mile or more inland. To guard against losing any of their supplies, Tim McCabe told his friends that it would be necessary to unload them themselves.

"From this p'int," said he, "we must hoe our own row ; under hiven we must depind on oursilves. Hardman, lind a hand there, and step lively."

To the astonishment of the youths, the man took hold and wrought with right good will. Jeff looked at Tim queerly as he pointed out the different articles, he himself, as may be said, overlooking the job; but the conclusion was that the Irishman had promised him a small amount for his help. When, however, the task was finished Tim came to the group, and while Hardman, with shamefaced expression, remained in the background, he said with that simplicity which any one would find hard to resist :

" You see poor Hardman is in bad luck ; he hain't any outfit, and wants to go to the gold fields, but will have to git some one to stake him. Obsarving the same, I made bowld to remark that it would give me frind Jiff the highest plisure to do it for him, not forgetting to obsarve that I knew his company would be agreeable to the byes, and he will be of great hilp to the same."

" Well, I'm blessed !" exclaimed the old miner, removing his hat and mopping his fore-head with his big red handkerchief. Then he turned half way round and looked steadily at the fellow, who was standing with his head down.

" Poor dog ! let him come along, but if he makes any trouble, I'll hold you responsible, Tim."

" And I'll be happy to take charge of the same 'sponsibility, and if he don't toe the mark,

it's mesilf that will make him. Do you hear
that, Ike?" he roared, turning fiercely toward
the fellow, who started, and meekly replied that
he heard, though it was impossible for anything to reach him except the last thunderous
demand.

" It isn't for us to say anything," remarked
Roswell aside to his chum, " but that means
trouble for us all."

" It surely does ; we must be on our guard
against him."

The outfits were piled on a sandspit about a
mile below the trading posts of Healy and
Wilson.   In the foreground were the ranch and
store owned by them, and beyond towered the
coast mountains, their tops gleaming in the
sunshine with enormous masses of snow, while
hundreds of miles still beyond stretched the immense Yukon country, toward which the eyes
of the civilized world are turned at the present
time.

One of the strange facts connected with
Alaska and the adjoining region is that in May
the sun rises at 3 o'clock and sets at 9, while in
June it rises at 1.30 and sets at 10.30.   Thus
the summer day is twenty hours long, and it

has a diffuse twilight. The change from winter to summer is rapid, winter setting in in September, and in the Klondike region zero weather lasts from November to May, though at times the weather moderates early in March, but does not become settled until May. The Yukon generally freezes shut in the latter part of October, and breaks up about the middle of May, when the western route to the gold fields by the river becomes practicable.

The hour was so late when our friends had finished carrying their outfit beyond reach of the high tide, which rises twenty feet at Dyea, that they lodged and took their meals at the ranch trading post. By arrangement, an early breakfast was eaten the next morning, and the goods were loaded upon the two Yukon sleds with which they were provided. These were seven feet long, sixteen inches wide, and were shod with steel. Other gold-seekers were stopping, like themselves, at the ranch, but they lagged so much that when the men and boys headed northward they were alone.

Jeff Graham and Ike Hardman passed the rope attached to one of the sleds over their shoulders, the elder in advance, and led off.

Tim took the lead, with the boys behind him, with the second sled, following the trail left by their friends. The deep snow was packed so hard that no use was made of the snow-shoes which Jeff had provided.

From Dyea the trail led for five miles over the ice, when they reached the mouth of the cañon. This is two miles long with an average width of fifty feet. The sleds were dragged over the strong ice, but later in the season, when it breaks up, travellers are obliged to follow the trail to the east of the cañon.

The party were so unaccustomed to this kind of labor that they found it exhausting. Curiously enough, Jeff bore the fatigue better than any. His iron muscles were the last to yield, and he was the first to resume the journey. He chaffed the others, and offered to let them mount his sled while he pulled them.

Beyond the cañon is a strip of woods three miles in length, which bears the name of Pleasant Camp, though it has not the first claim to the name. It does not contain the ruins of even a cabin or shanty—nothing, in fact, but trees, through which the wintry winds sough and howl dismally. There the party halted, ate lunch, rested for an hour, and then set out with the determination to make the next camping ground before night.

The ascent now became gradual, and before the day was spent they arrived at Sheep Camp, on the edge of the timber. This is the last spot where wood for fuel can be obtained until the other side of Chilkoot Pass is reached. The tent was pitched on top of the snow, the poles and pins being shoved down into it. Jeff took it upon himself to cut what fuel was needed, gathering at the same time a liberal quantity of hemlock brush, upon which to spread their blankets for beds.

Since it was necessary to use the stove, and it must rest on the snow, a simple arrangement provided against trouble from the melting of the latter. Three poles, eight feet in length, were laid parallel on the snow and the stove placed upon them. Although a hole was soon dissolved beneath, the length of the supports kept the stove upright.

The experience which Jeff and Tim had had made them both excellent cooks, which was a fortunate thing for the boys, since they would have made sorry work in preparing a meal; but

THE TENT POLES WERE SHOVED DOWN INTO THE SNOW.

the art of the Irishman deserved the many compliments it received. With the aid of baking powder he prepared a goodly number of light, flaky biscuit, and by exposing some of the butter to the warmth of the stove, it was gradually changed from its stone-like hardness to a consistency that permitted it to be cut with a knife and spread upon the hot bread. The coffee was amber, clear, and fragrant, and with the condensed milk and sugar would have reflected credit upon the *chef* of any establishment. In addition, there were fried bacon and canned corn.

Until this time the boys had never believed they could eat bacon, but nothing could have had a more delicious flavor to them. It was not alone because of their vigorous appetites, but partly on account of the bitterly cold weather. There is a good deal of animal heat evolved in the digestion of fat bacon, and it is therefore among the favorite articles of food in the Arctic regions.

Probably there isn't a boy in the country who would not revolt at the thought of eating a tallow candle, and yet if he was exposed to the rigors of Greenland and the far north, he would soon look upon it as one of the greatest delicacies of the table.

The hemlock branches were now spread on top of the snow at the side of the tent, a large square of canvas was placed over them, upon which the blankets and robes were put, the whole forming a springy, comfortable bed.

Roswell and Frank were sure that in all their lives they were never so tired. Leaving the three men to talk and smoke, they stretched out on their blankets, wrapping themselves in them, and almost immediately sank into deep, dreamless slumber.

The sleep had lasted perhaps a couple of hours, when, without any apparent cause, Frank Mansley awoke in the full possession of his senses. Lying motionless, he listened to the soft breathing of his cousin beside him, while the regular respiration of the men left no doubt of their condition. Everything around was in blank, impenetrable darkness and all profoundly still.

" It's strange that I should awake like this," he thought, slightly shifting his position. " I'm tired, and was so drowsy that I felt as if

I could sleep a week, but I was never wider awake than I am this minute—"

Amid the all-pervading silence he was sensible of a low, solemn murmur, like that of the distant ocean. At first it seemed to be the " voice of silence" itself, but it steadily increased in volume until its roar became overpowering. Startled and frightened, he lay still, wondering what it could mean, or whether his senses were deceiving him. Then he suddenly remembered the vast masses of ice and snow which towered above them all through the day. He recalled the stories he had read of the glaciers and avalanches, and how Tim McCabe had referred to them as sometimes overtaking travellers in this part of the world.

He knew what it meant, and, leaping from his couch, he shouted :

" Wake up ! Quick ! An avalanche is upon us !"

CHAPTER V.

THROUGH CHILKOOT PASS.

As Frank Mansley's words rang through the tent they were followed by the awful roar of the descending avalanche, and all awoke on the instant. But no one could do anything to save himself. They could only cower and pray to Heaven to protect them.

Something struck the side of the tent, like the plunge of a mountain torrent, yet it was not that, nor was it the snow. Tim McCabe knew its nature, and catching his breath, he called :

"It's the wind of the avalanche ! That won't hurt ye !"

The wonder was that it did not blow the canvas like a feather from its path; but the tent held its position, and the appalling rush and roar ceased with more suddenness than it had begun. The throbbing air became still.

Jeff Graham, who had not spoken, struck a

match, and holding it above his head, peered around the interior of the tent, which he observed had sagged a good deal from the impact of the avalanche's breath, though the stakes held their places in the snow. He saw Frank Mansley standing pale with affright, while Roswell, sitting on the edge of his couch, was equally startled. Ike Hardman had covered his face with his blanket, like a child, who thus seeks to escape an impending danger. Incredible as it may seem, Tim McCabe was filling his pipe in the gloom, preparatory to a smoke.

" Be aisy," was his comment, as he struck a match and held it above the bowl ; " we're as safe as if in 'Frisco, and a little safer, for it's whin ye are there ye are liable to have an airthquake tumble the buildings about yer hid."

" Wasn't that an avalanche?" asked the amazed Frank.

" It was that, but it didn't hit us. If we had put up the tint a little beyant and further to the right, we'd've been mashed flat."

He spoke the truth. The enormous mass of snow, weighing thousands of tons, had toppled over and slid down the mountain-side with a roar like Niagara, but stopped short, just before reaching the tent. Some of the feathery particles sailed forward and struck the canvas, the greatest effect being produced by the wind, but the monster was palsied before he could reach forward and seize his victims.

When the situation became clear, every one uttered expressions of gratitude, but the boys were not relieved of all fear. What had taken place might occur again.

"Not a bit of it," was Tim's reassuring reply. "I've obsarved the things before, and we shan't be bothered agin to-night. Take me advice and go to sleep, which the same is what I shall do mesilf as soon as I finishes me smoke."

The shock, however, had been too great for all to compose their nerves at once. Jeff was the first to succumb, having faith in the assurance of his friend, and Ike Hardman soon followed him in the land of dreams. Frank and Roswell lay for a long time talking in low tones, but finally drowsiness overcame them, and with the pungent odor of Tim's pipe in their nostrils they sank into slumber, which was not broken until Jeff called to them that breakfast was waiting.

The melted snow furnished what water they needed to drink and in which to lave their faces and hands. Then, before eating, they hurried outside the tent to survey the snowy mountain that had come so near swallowing them up. They were filled with amazement when they looked upon the vast pile, amid which were observed many chunks and masses of ice, several that must have weighed hundreds of pounds, lying on the snow within a few yards of the tent. Had one of these been precipitated against the shelter, it would have crushed the inmates, like the charge from the most enormous of our seacoast guns. It was a providential escape, indeed, for our friends, and it was no wonder that they continued to discuss it and to express their gratitude to Heaven, that had mercifully shielded them while they slept.

Standing at Sheep Camp, they saw the summit towering thirty-five hundred feet in front, though Chilkoot Pass, which they were to follow, is five hundred feet lower. The task of climbing to the summit of this pass is of the most trying nature conceivable, and many gold-seekers have turned back in despair. Terrific weather is often encountered, and men have been held in camp for weeks, during which the crest of the mountains was hidden by clouds and tempests, and the whirling snow and sleet were **so** blinding that they hardly ventured to **peep** out from their tent. The weather was such as has baffled the most intrepid of explorers for centuries in their search for the North Pole.

Our friends were unusually fortunate in being favored with good weather, there being hardly any wind stirring, while, more wonderful than all, the sun shone from an unclouded sky, in a section where the clear days average less than seventy degrees in the course of the entire year.

No one who has ever climbed Chilkoot Pass will forget it. Some, alas! who have made the attempt never succeeded in reaching the other side, but perished in the frightful region; while many more have become disheartened by the perils and difficulties and turned back when on the threshold of the modern El Dorado. At the foot of the pass our friends met two men, bending low with the packs strapped to their shoulders, and plodding wearily southward. Tim called to them to know what the trouble was, and received a glum answer, accompanied by an oath that they had had enough of such a country, and if they ever lived to reach New York, they would shoot any man who pronounced the word " Klondike" in their presence.

It is a curious fact regarding this famous pass that the snow with which it is choked is what makes it possible for travel. The snow sometimes lies to the depth of fifty or sixty feet, and from February, through May, and often June, its smooth surface allows one to walk over it without trouble. Should it be fine and yielding, the snow-shoes come into play, but when the crust is hard, no better support could be asked. The trouble lies in the steep incline, which becomes more decided the higher one climbs.

Underneath this enormous mass rush violent torrents of water, which, hollowing out passages for themselves, leave the snow white arches far above, over which one walks upon a natural bridge. Later in the season, when the effects of the warm weather are felt, these arches begin to tumble in, and the incautious traveller who misses his footing and drops into one of the huge crevices is lost.

As has been said, the steepness increases as
one approaches the top, the last five hundred
feet being like the roof of a house.   Bending
forward under their loads, our friends often
found their noses within a few inches of the
snow, while masses of rock protruding in many
places added to the difficulties of travel.   The
combined strength of the party was required to
get a single sled to the top.   While one was
left behind, they joined in pushing and pulling
the other, with frequent pauses for rest, until,
after hours of the hardest work conceivable,
they succeeded in reaching the summit.   Then,
resting again, they began their descent for the
other sled.   It was fortunate that the crust of
the snow removed the need of using the long
snow-shoes, whose make suggests the bats used
in playing tennis, for the men were the only
ones who knew how to handle the awkward
contrivances, which would have proved a sore
perplexity for Roswell and Frank.

Under some circumstances it becomes a question which is the harder, to descend or ascend a
steep hill.   Despite the utmost care, the whole
five stumbled several times.   Roswell felt the
chills run through him, and he held his breath

ALL JOINED IN PUSHING AND PULLING ONE SLED.

in dismay when he saw himself sliding toward the edge of a ravine, over which if he fell he would have been dashed to death on the instant. While desperately trying to check himself, he shouted for help, but it looked equally fatal for any one to venture near him, since the slope was so abrupt that he could not check himself.

Jeff Graham was carrying the coil of rope which he had loosened from the first sled, and, seeing the peril of his young friend, he flung the end toward him with the skill of a Mexican or cowboy in throwing the *rita*, or lasso. The youth was slipping downward on his face, with his terrified countenance turned appealingly to his friends, while he tried, by jamming his toes and clutching at the surface, to check himself, and Frank was on the point of going to his help when the end of the rope struck his shoulder and he seized it with both hands. The next minute he was drawn back to safety.

"I'm surprised wid ye," remarked Tim McCabe, when the panting youth stood among them again. "I thought ye were too tired to indulge in any such foolin'. Whin ye want to slide down hill, make use of the slid instead of your stummick."

" I don't think I'll want to do any more slid
ing down hill in this part of the world," replied
the frightened, but grateful youth.

Once more they bent to their work, and pulling themselves together, succeeded at last in
reaching the summit with the second sled, the
whole party utterly used up. Even Jeff
Graham sat down on one of the loads, panting
and too tired to speak. When he found voice,
he said :

" What fools we are ! And yet if I went
back to 'Frisco, I'd start agin for the Klondike
the next day ; so I reckon we'll keep on."

No one responded, for they were so wearied
that talking itself was labor.

Looking to the southwest, they could see the
blue shimmer of the Pacific, where the Gulf of
Alaska rolls its white surges against the dismal
shores. Far in the distance a faint line against
the sky showed where a steamer was probably
ploughing its way to St. Michael's, with hundreds of gold-seekers on board, the van of the
army that is pushing toward the Klondike
from the West, the South, and the East, until
it would seem that even that immense region
must overflow with the innumerable multitudes,

drawn thither by the most resistless magnet that can make men brave peril, suffering, and death.

Turning in the opposite direction, they saw the mountain slope melting away in the great valley of the Yukon, with the trail leading through a narrow, rocky gap, and with naked granite rocks rising steeply to the partly snow-clad mountains. The party had been fortunate in completing the ascent in less than a day, when it often requires twice as long. The first half mile of the descent was steep, when the slope becomes more gradual. The glare of the snow compelled all to use their glasses, and seven miles from the summit they reached the edge of timber, where camp was made.

Freed from all fear of descending avalanches, with plenty of food and wood for fuel, the exhausted gold-hunters lay down on their blankets, resting upon more hemlock boughs, and enjoyed the most refreshing sleep since leaving the steamer at Juneau. It was not until considerably after daylight that Jeff awoke and started a new fire, with which to prepare their breakfast, and when that was ready the boys were roused from slumber.

They were now within three miles of Lake
Lindeman, a body of water five miles in length,
and the journey was speedily made. It was
on the shore of this lake that the party expected
to build a raft or boat with which to make the
long, rough voyage to the Yukon, but, to their
pleased surprise, they found an old Indian, with
a broad scow, anxious to transport them and
their luggage to the foot of the lake. He had
already secured three men and their outfits,
but was able to carry the new arrivals, and
Jeff was not long in making a bargain with
him.

CHAPTER VI.

A SIGNIFICANT DISCOVERY.

GAME is so scarce in the valley of the Upper Yukon and in the Klondike country that many gold-seekers take no firearms at all with them. Years ago the Indians showed occasional hostility toward the missions and trading-posts, but nothing now is to be feared from them. They are often hired to help carry loads through the passes, and with that aptitude for imitating the white man, they have speedily learned to charge high prices for their labor.

Before leaving Juneau, Jeff Graham presented each of his little party with an excellent revolver, quoting the remark which a cowboy once made to a tenderfoot :

" You may not want the weapon often, but when you do you'll want it mighty bad."

Jeff took with him his own pistol which he had carried for years, besides which he was provided with a fine Winchester rifle.   He knew he was not likely to find any use for it in shooting game, but he grimly observed that if a pistol should prove handy, the larger weapon was apt to prove much more so.

The Indian who engaged to take them to the foot of Lake Lindeman was old, but wiry and tough, and understood his business. He could speak a few words of English, which were enough for his purposes. He raised a small soiled sail of canvas on the scow, and with the help of a long pole kept the heavily laden craft moving. Although the lake was open thus early in the season, the shores were lined with ice, much of it extending into the water for a number of rods. Huge cakes sometimes bumped against the scow, but they caused no damage, and did not interfere with its progress.

The three men who had first engaged the boat looked as if they had come a long distance. Our friends had no recollection of having seen them on the steamer from Seattle or on the steam launch that connects Juneau with Dyea at the head of Lynn Canal. Where they came from, therefore, was a mystery, the probability being that they had been loitering about Dyea for a long time, waiting for the season to advance sufficiently to allow them to start for the Yukon. They seemed reserved to the point of sullenness, keeping by themselves and showing so much antipathy to any approach that they were let alone.

But just before the foot of the lake, nearly six miles distant, was reached, Frank Mansley made an interesting discovery. The most ill-favored of the trio was an acquaintance of Ike Hardman. No one else noticed the significant fact, and it was partly through accident that the truth came to the lad.

The two men acted as if strangers, not exchanging a word on the passage, and seemingly feeling no interest in each other. All of Frank's friends were near the bow of the boat, looking to where they were soon to touch shore. Two of the strangers were standing just back of and near them, while Hardman was in the middle of the boat, apparently watching the old Indian as he plied his paddle with untiring vigor.

The third stranger was at the stern, seated on the gunwale, smoking a clay pipe and seemingly taking no note of anything about him. When Ike Hardman sauntered among the piles of luggage to the rear, Frank was impelled by an impulse for which he could not account to watch him. He had no well-defined suspicion, and least of all did he suspect what proved to be the truth.

Hardman halted a few paces from the man sitting on the edge of the boat, and, so far as appearances went, did not pay any attention to him. A quick, furtive glance to the front put the lad on his guard, and he, too, turned his face toward land, but his position was such that he could look sideways at the two, while not seeming to do so.

Suddenly Hardman, with his back partly toward the youth, made a sign with his hands, the meaning of which Frank could not catch, because the signal was not fully seen, but the fellow sitting down nodded his head, and taking his pipe from between his lips, said something in so guarded a voice that only the ears for which the words were intended could understand them.

This brief interchange ought to have been enough, but Hardman did not appear to think so. He stepped somewhat closer, and he, too, spoke, still gesticulating with one of his hands. The man addressed was impatient. He nodded again in a jerky fashion, and made answer

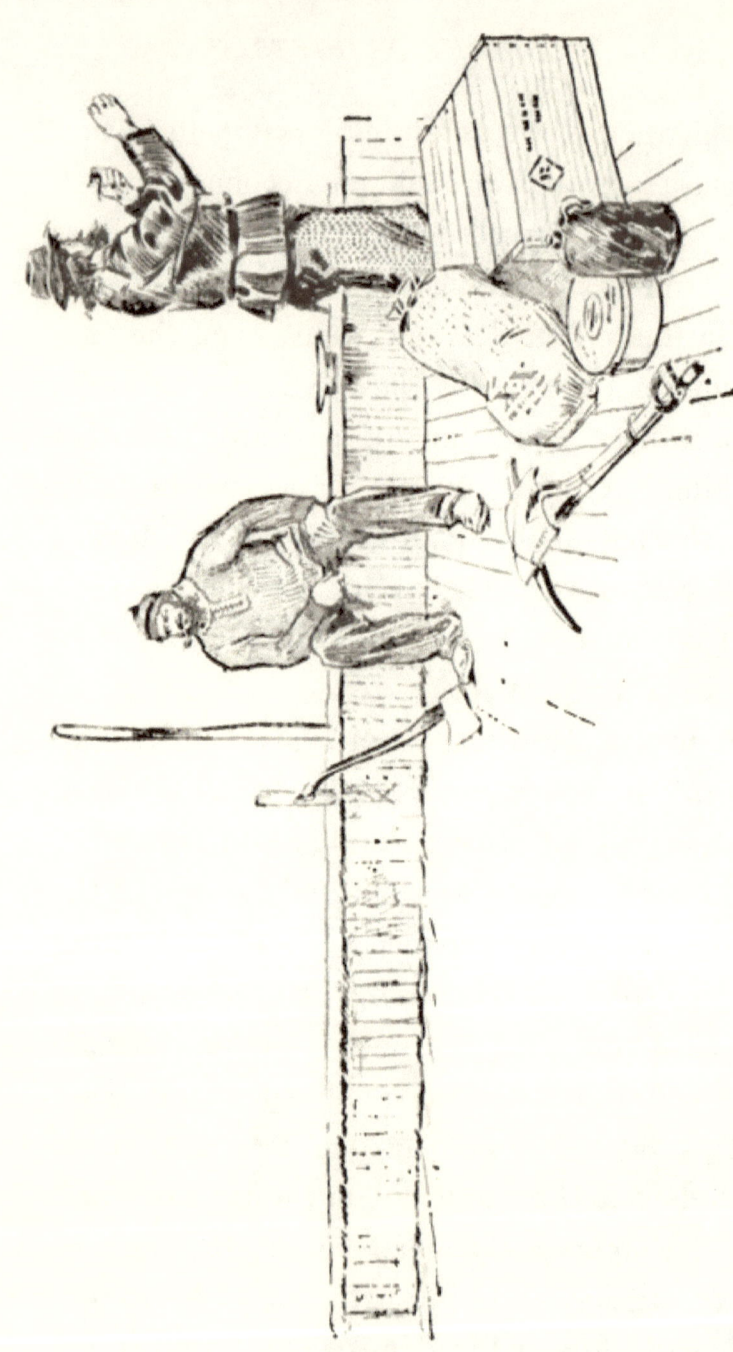

SUDDENLY HARDMAN MADE A SIGN.

with less caution, as a consequence of which the eavesdropper caught the words, " Yes, yes, to-night ; I understand."

Hardman was satisfied, and came back to the front of the boat, which was now approaching the shore. His friend smoked a few minutes until the scow bumped against the projection of ice, and, the old Indian leaping lightly out, carried the heavy stone anchor as far as the rope would permit. This held the boat in place, and the unloading began. The Indian offered to help for an extravagant price, but his offer was refused, and the respective parties busied themselves with their own work.

The discovery made by Frank Mansley caused him considerable uneasiness. The dislike which he felt toward Hardman the first time he saw him had never abated, and it was the same with his cousin. Young as they were, they felt that a great mistake was made when Hardman was allowed to join the party, and they wondered that Jeff permitted it, but, as has been shown, they were too discreet to object.

That Hardman, on his part, detested the youths was apparent, though he tried to conceal the feeling when he feared it might attract the attention of others. He had little to say to them or they to him. Frank decided to tell his chum of the discovery he had made, and they would consult as to whether they should take Jeff and Tim into their confidence.

Meanwhile, the trio gathered their loads upon their backs and started northward without so much as calling good-by to those whom they left behind, and who were not sorry to part company with them.

The gold-hunters had had a little lift on their journey, but it was not worth considering, in view of what remained before them. A mile advance with sleds and their packs took them to the head of Lake Bennet, where it may be said the navigation of the Yukon really begins. The lake is about twenty-eight miles long, contains a number of islands, and in going to the foot one passes from Alaska into British Columbia. Along its shores were scores of miners, busily engaged in building boats with which to make the rest of the journey. Sad to say, owing to their impatience and lack of skill, some of the boats were so flimsy and ill-constructed that they were certain to go to pieces in the fierce rapids below, and add their owners to the long list of victims whose bodies strew the pathway from Chilkoot to the Upper Yukon.

Here, too, it became necessary for our friends to build a craft, and since it was comparatively early in the day, Jeff and Tim, each with an axe over his shoulder, went into the wood, already partly cut down, Hardman accompanying them, in order to bear his turn. The boys remained behind to guard the property, though their neighbors were so occupied with their own affairs that they gave them little heed. Frank took the opportunity to tell his companion what he had observed on the boat while crossing the lake.

" Hardman has joined our company for some evil purpose," said Roswell, " and the other man is his partner in the plot."

" But they are gone, and we may not see them again."

" One of them, at least, has an understanding with Hardman, and will keep him within hailing distance."

" We will say nothing to Jeff or Tim until to-morrow ; I fear that we shall learn something to-night."

The boy was right in his supposition.

CHAPTER VII.

THE PLOTTERS.

ALL day long the two axes swung vigorously. Both Jeff and Tim were expert woodmen, and they felled pine after pine. Hardman pleaded that he was unaccustomed to such work ; but Jeff grimly told him he could never have a better chance to learn to cut down trees, and compelled him to take his turn. The work was continued until dark, which, it will be remembered, comes much later in the far North than in our latitude.

The distance between the scene of their work and the point where the outfits and goods were piled was so slight that there was really no need of the boys remaining on guard. Feeling that they were favored too much, they sauntered to the wood and asked the privilege of taking a hand in felling the trees. It was granted ; but they made such sorry work, finding it almost impossible to sink the blade twice in the same spot, that they yielded the implements to those who understood the business so much better.

The snow was deep, and the camp was much the same as the one made before entering Chilkoot Pass. All were tired, and lay down after the evening meal, glad of the opportunity for a few hours' sleep.

In accordance with their agreement, the boys said nothing to either of their friends about what Frank had observed on the boat. It was understood between them that they were to feign sleep, but to keep watch of Hardman during the night as long as they could remain awake. Ordinarily it is a difficult if not impossible task for one to fight off the insidious approach of slumber, but Frank Mansley had wrought himself into such a state of anxiety that he was sure he could command his senses until well toward morning.

He and Roswell lay under the same blanket, with their backs to each other, while the others were by themselves, the interior of the tent barely permitting the arrangement. Had any one stealthily entered fifteen minutes after they had lain down, he would have declared that all were asleep, though such was not the fact.

Despite his nervousness, Frank was beginning to feel drowsy when he was startled and set on edge by a sound that penetrated the profound silence. It resembled the whistle of a bird from the timber, soft, clear, and tremulous. Almost in the same instant he heard one of the men rise stealthily from his couch. It was easy to determine, from the direction of the slight rustle, that it was Hardman.

Frank thrust his elbow into the back of his comrade as a warning for him to be alert ; but there was no response. Roswell had been asleep for an hour. It was too dark to perceive anything within the tent, though all was clear outside ; but the lad's senses were in that tense condition that he heard the man lift the flap of the tent and move softly over the snow on the outside. With the same silence, Frank flung back the blanket that enveloped him and stepped out on the packed snow of the interior. Pausing but a moment, he crept through the opening. In that cold region men sleep in their clothing, so he had nothing to fear from exposure.

The night was brilliantly clear, the sky studded with stars, and not a breath of air stirring. He remained a brief while in a crouching posture, while he peered in different directions. Before him stretched the lake, its shores crusted with snow and ice, with the cold water shining in the star-gleam. Still stooping low and looking intently about him, he saw something move between the tent and the water. A second glance revealed Hardman, who was standing alone and looking about him, as if he expected the approach of some person. Impatient at the delay, he repeated the signal that had aroused the attention of Frank a few minutes before.

The tremulous note had scarcely pierced the air when a shadowy form emerged from the wood and walked the short distance that took him to the waiting Hardman. The two were so far off that it was impossible to identify him ; but the lad was as certain it was the man who had exchanged the words and signs with Hardman as if the noonday sun were shining.

Frank Mansley would have given anything he had to be able to steal near enough to overhear what passed between them, but that was clearly impossible. To move from his place by the tent was certain to bring instant detection. Now and then he could catch the faint murmur of their voices, but not once was he able to distinguish a syllable that was uttered.

The interview lasted but a short time. Whatever understanding was reached between the plotters must have been simple, else it would not have been effected so soon. Suddenly the stranger moved off over the snow in the direction of the wood and disappeared among the trees. At the same moment Hardman moved silently toward the tent. Frank was on the alert, and when the man entered he was lying on his couch, his blanket over him, and his chilled body against the warm form of his comrade, who recoiled slightly with a shiver, though he did not awake.

The fear of Frank Mansley had been that the two men were plotting some scheme for the robbery of Jeff, though it would seem that they would prefer to wait until he had made a strike in the gold district. What the youth had seen convinced him that the latter plan would be followed, or at least attempted, and he had

"YOU'RE A PRETTY FELLOW TO STAND GUARD," SAID FRANK.

hardly reached that conclusion when he fell asleep.

" You're a pretty fellow to stand guard," he remarked to his cousin the next morning, after the men had gone to the wood again.

" I didn't try to stand guard," replied Roswell with a laugh ; " I was lying down all the time."

" Why didn't you keep awake ?"

" Because I fell asleep, and you would have done the same if you hadn't kept awake."

" Probably I should—most people do ; but what do you think of it, Roswell ?"

" First tell me something to think of."

His cousin told all that he had seen the night before.

" There can't be any doubt that Hardman and one, if not all three of those fellows, are plotting mischief. It might have been one of the others who signalled to and met him. I think we ought to tell Jeff."

" We'll do so before night. It isn't likely Hardman suspects anything, and you will have no trouble in finding the chance."

" You think it best that I should tell Jeff ?"

" By all means, since you will tell what you

saw. Such things are best first-hand ; but neither of us will say anything to Tim."

" Why not ?"

" Jeff is the leader of this expedition. Tim is so soft-hearted that likely enough he would try to convince Hardman of his wrongdoing, and so put him on his guard. Let Jeff tell him if he chooses."

" I hope he will drive Hardman out of our party ; my impression of him is that he would not only rob but kill for the sake of gold."

Roswell looked grave. The same thought had been in his mind, but he disliked to give expression to it. He hoped his cousin was wrong, but could not feel certain that he was.

" Frank, make an excuse for calling Jeff here ; he ought to know of this at once."

Looking toward the timber, they saw that their friend had just given up his axe to Hardman, who was swinging it a short distance from where Tim McCabe was lustily doing the same. Frank called to him, and when the old miner looked around, he beckoned for him to approach. Jeff slouched forward, wondering why the boys had summoned him from his work. He was quickly told. He listened, silent, but deeply interested, until the story was finished. Then, without any excitement, he said, " Don't let Tim know anything of this, younkers ;" and, with a strange gleam in his keen gray eyes, the old man added, " I've got a Winchester and a revolver, and I keep 'em both loaded, and I've plenty of ammunition. I think I'll have use for 'em purty soon."

CHAPTER VIII.

THE men wrought steadily in felling trees, and by the close of the second day had enough timber for their raft. It would have been much preferable could they have constructed a good, stout boat; but it was not feasible, though Jeff and Tim would have built it had they possessed the necessary planking and boards. They had provided themselves with oakum, pitch, and other material; but the labor of sawing out the right kind of stuff would have taken weeks. The Irishman had learned from his late experience; as a result of which a double-decker, as it may be termed, was planned. This consisted first of a substantial framework of buoyant pine logs, securely nailed together, while upon that was reared another some two feet in height. This upper framework was intended to bear their outfits, over which were fastened rubber cloths. The Alaskan lakes are often swept by terrific tempests, the waves sometimes dashing entirely over the rafts and boats, and wetting everything that is not well protected. The upper deck serves also partially to protect the men.

The boys spent a portion of the days in fishing. There was a notable moderation in the weather, the snow and ice rapidly melting. Sitting or standing on the bank, they cast out their lines, baited with bits of meat, and met with pleasing success. Plump, luscious white-fish, grayling, and lake trout were landed in such numbers that little or no other solid food was eaten during their halt at the head of Lake Bennet.

Work was pushed so vigorously that on the third day the goods were carefully piled on the upper deck, secured in place, and with their long poles they pushed out from the shore on the voyage of twenty-eight miles to the foot of the sheet of water. They were provided with a sturdy mast reared near the middle of the craft, but they did not erect a sail, for the reason that the strong wind which was blowing was almost directly from the north, and would have checked their progress.

The unwieldy structure was pushed along

the eastern side, where the poles were service-
able at all times. Each took his turn at the
work, the boys with the others, and the progress, if slow, was sure.

The first twelve miles of Lake Bennet are
quite shallow, with a width barely exceeding a
half mile. Fifteen miles down occurs the junction with the southwest arm, and the point had
hardly come into sight when Tim said:

" Now look out for trouble, for here's where
we'll catch it sure."

All understood what he meant, for a wind
was blowing down the arm with such fierce-
ness that it looked as if everything would be
swept off the raft. The prospect was so threatening that they ran inshore while yet at a safe
distance, and waited for the gale to subside.

" Is it likely to last long ?" asked Roswell,
when they had secured shelter.

" That depinds how far off the end of the
same may be," was the unsatisfactory reply.
" I've knowed men to be held here for days,
but I have hopes that we may get off in the
coorse of two or three weeks."

The boys as well as Jeff could not believe
that Tim was in earnest, for his lightest words

were often spoken with the gravest expression of face ; but their former experience taught them to be prepared for almost any whim in the weather. They recalled those dismal days and nights earlier on their journey, when they were storm-stayed, and they were depressed at the thought that something of the nature might again overtake them. When the boys proposed to put up the tent, the Irishman said :

"It is early in the day ; bide awhile before going to that trouble."

This remark convinced them that he was more hopeful of a release than would be implied from his words ; so they wrapped their heavy coats closer and hoped for the best. The men lit their pipes, while the boys huddled close together and had little to say. Unexpectedly there came such a lull in the gale early in the afternoon that the voyage, to the delight of all, was resumed.

Ike Hardman was in more genial spirits than at any time since he joined the company. He showed an eagerness to help, declining to yield the pole when Jeff offered to relieve him, and ventured now and then upon some jest with Roswell and Frank. Their distrust, however, was not lessened, and they were too honest to affect a liking that it was impossible to feel. They had little to say to him, and noticing the fact, he finally let them alone. Whatever misgiving Jeff may have felt was skilfully concealed, and the fellow could have felt no suspicion that his secret was suspected by any member of the company.

The wind blew so strongly that there was some misgiving ; but observing that it came from the right quarter, the sail was hoisted, and as the canvas bellied outward, the raft caught the impulse and began moving through the water at a rate that sent the ripples flying over the square ends of the logs at the front. All sat down on the upper framework, with the exception of Jeff, who stood, pole in hand, at the bow, ready to guide the structure should it sheer in the wrong direction.

The conformation of the shore and a slight change of wind carried the raft farther out on the lake. Observing that it was getting slightly askew, Jeff pushed the long pole downward until his hand almost touched the surface of the water. While holding it there the other end bobbed up, having failed to touch ground.

" No use," he said, facing his friends, who were watching him, " the bottom may be half a mile below."

" That looks as if we're over our hids," said Tim; " by which token, if this steamer blows up we've got to swim for our lives, and I never larned to swim a stroke."

The boys looked at him wonderingly.

" How is it you did not learn ?" asked Roswell.

" I've tried hundreds of times. I kept in the water till me toes begun to have webs between 'em, but at the first stroke me hid went down and me heels up. I can swim in that style," he added gravely, " but find the same slightly inconvanient owing to the necissity of braithing now and thin. I tried fur a long time to braithe through me toes, but niver made much of a succiss of it."

" And I learned to swim in one day," remarked Frank ; " strange that you should have so much trouble."

" Undoubtedly that's because yer hid is so light, while me own brains weigh me down ; it's aisy to understand that."

" If we should have any mishap, Tim," said

Frank, " you must remember to hold fast to a piece of wood to help you float—a small bit is enough."

" I have a bitter plan than that."

" What is it ?"

" Niver have anything to do wid the water."

" That would be certain safety if you could carry it out ; but you can't help it all times – such, for instance, as the present."

" And I'm thinking we shall have plinty of the same before we raich Dawson."

" After we get to the foot of this lake, what comes next, Tim ?"

" Caribou Crossing, which we pass through to Lake Tagish, which isn't quite as big as is this one. I'm thinking," he added thoughtfully, watching the rising anger of the waves, " that bime-by, whin we come near land, we'll be going that fast that we'll skim over the snow like a sled to the nixt lake."

Roswell pointed to the shore on their right, indicating a stake which rose upright from the ground and stood close to the water.

" What is the meaning of that ?" he asked.

" That," replied Tim, " marks the grave of some poor chap that died on his way to the

"OH, LOOK THERE! ISN'T IT DREADFUL?"

Klondike. Do ye obsarve that cairn of stones a bit beyont ?"

Each saw it.

" That marks anither grave ; and ye may call to mind that we obsarved more of the same along Lake Lindeman."

Such was the fact, though this was the first reference to them.

"And we shall hardly be out of sight of some of the same all the way to the Klondike ; and I'm thinking," was his truthful remark, " that hundreds more will lay their bones down in these parts and niver see their loved ones again."

It was a sad thought. In a few years improved routes, railway-tracks, and houses for food and lodging will rob the Klondike region of its terrors, but until then death must exact a heavy toll from the gold-seekers crowding northward, without regard to season or the simplest laws of prudence.

Roswell was standing on the upper deck, near a corner, when he exclaimed excitedly:

" Oh, look there ! Isn't it dreadful ?"

He was pointing out on the lake, and, following the direction of his hand, all saw the answer to his question.

CHAPTER IX.

ALL hurried to the side of Roswell, who was pointing to a place a short distance from the raft.

It was the body of a man that they saw, floating face upward. His clothing was good, and the white features, partly hidden by a black beard, must have been pleasing in life. The feet and hands, dangling at the sides, were so low in the water that only when stirred by the waves did they show, but the face rose and fell, sometimes above, and never more than a few inches below, so that it was in view all the time.

The group silently viewed the scene. The body drifted nearer and nearer and faintly touched the edge of the raft, as the wind carried it past. Then it continued dipping, and gradually floated away in the gathering gloom.

"We ought to give it burial," said Frank to Jeff, who shook his head.

" What's the use ? We might tow it ashore, dig up a foot of the frozen earth, and set a wooden cross or heap of stones to mark the grave, but the lake is as good a burial-place as it could have."

" I wonder who he could have been," said Roswell thoughtfully. " Some man, no doubt, who has come from his home in the States, thousands of miles away, and started to search for gold. He may have left wife and children behind, who will look longingly for his coming, but will never see his face again."

" The world is full of such sad things," observed Tim McCabe, impressed, like all, with the melancholy incident, and then he expressed the thought that was in the mind of each: " There be five of us : will we all see home again ?"

There was no reply. Hardman had not spoken, and, as if the occasion was too oppressive, he sauntered to another part of the raft, while the rest gradually separated, each grave and saddened by what he had witnessed.

It is well for us to turn aside from the hurly-burly of life and reflect upon the solemn fact of the inevitable end that awaits us all.

But the long afternoon was drawing to a close, and the question to be considered was whether the raft should be allowed to drift or land, or they should continue forward, despite a certain degree of danger during the darkness. All were eager to improve the time, and Jeff, as the head of the expedition, said they would keep at it at least for a while longer.

" As far as I can tell," he said, " there's no danger of running into anything that'll wreck us, and we must use our sail while we can. Besides," he added, after testing it, " the water is so deep that we can't reach bottom, and there isn't much chance to help ourselves."

The wind which swept over the raft had risen almost to a gale, and brought with it a few scurrying flakes of snow. There was a perceptible fall in the temperature, and the chilly, penetrating air caused all to shiver, despite their thick clothing.

Finally night closed in, and the raft was still drifting, the wind carrying it four or five miles an hour. The night was so short that the hope was general that the straightforward progress would continue until sunrise, though Tim, who was better acquainted with the region, expressed the belief that a storm of several days' duration had set in.

Since there was nothing to do, the men and boys disposed of themselves as comfortably as possible on the lee side of the raft, beyond reach of the waves, though the spray now and then dashed against their rubber blankets which each had wrapped about his shoulders and body. After a time Jeff took his station at the bow, though an almost imperceptible change of wind caused the structure to drift partly sideways.

Roswell and Frank, who were seated back to back and in an easy attitude, had sunk into a doze, when both were startled by a bump which swung them partly over. They straightened up and looked around in the gloom, wondering what it meant.

"We've struck shore," called Jeff, who was the only one on watch. "The voyage is over for the time."

There was hurrying to and fro, as all perceived that he had spoken the truth. The corner of the raft had impinged against some ice that was piled on the beach. The gloom was too deep for any one to see more than a few rods, so that Tim, who had traversed the sheet of water before, was unable to guess where they were.

" Provided we've come over a straight coorse," said the Irishman, " we can't be far from the fut of the lake."

" We'll know in the morning, which can't be far off," replied Jeff ; " we'll make ourselves as comfortable as we can until then."

Despite the wind, they managed to light several matches and examine their watches. To their surprise, the night was nearly gone, and it was decided not to attempt to put up their tent until daylight. Accordingly, they huddled together and spent the remaining hour of gloom in anything but comfort.

At the earliest streakings of light all were astir. Springing from the ground, Tim McCabe hurriedly walked a short way to the northward. The others had risen to their feet and were watching him. As the gray light rapidly overspread the scene, they saw the lake, still tossing with whitecaps, stretching to the south and west, with the shore faintly visible. On the east, north, south, and west towered the snow-capped mountains, with Mount Lotne and

"WE'RE AT THE FUT OF THE LAKE," SHOUTED TIM.

other peaks piercing the very clouds. The sun was still hidden, with the air damp, cold, and penetrating.

Tim McCabe was seen to stand motionless for some minutes, when he slowly turned about on his heels and attentively studied the landmarks. Then he suddenly flung his cap high in air, and, catching it as it came down, began dancing a jig with furious vigor. He acted as if he had bidden good-by to his senses.

" Whoop! hurrah !" he shouted, as he replaced his cap and hurried to his friends. " We're at the fut of the lake !"

Such was the fact. A steamer guided by pilot and compass could not have come more directly to the termination of the sheet of water. Tim had cause for rejoicing, and all congratulated themselves upon their good fortune.

" There's only one bad thing about the same," he added more seriously.

" What's that ?" asked Jeff.

" We're no longer in the United States."

" That's the fact," said Hardman, " we're in British Columbia."

After all, this was a small matter. Inasmuch as the signs indicated a severe storm, it was decided to stay where they were until its chief fury was spent. The snow was shovelled aside to allow them to reach the frozen earth, into which the stakes were securely driven, and the tent set up, with the stove in position.

Beyond Chilkoot Pass plenty of timber is to be found, consisting of pine, spruce, cottonwood, and birch. Thus far not the first sign of game had been seen. The whole country, after leaving Dyea, is mountainous.

Most of the goods were left on the raft, where they were protected by the rubber sheathing and the secure manner in which they were packed and bound.

Three dreary days of waiting followed, and the hours became so monotonous at times, especially after the hard, active toil that had preceded them, that in some respects it was the most trying period of the memorable journey of our friends from Dyea to Dawson City. The men found consolation in their pipes, which frequently made the air within the tent intolerable to the youngsters. Like most smokers, however, the men never suspected the annoyance they caused, and the boys were too considerate to hint anything of the kind. When their young limbs yearned for exercise, they bolted out of doors, in the face of the driving sleet and fine snow which cut the face like bird-shot. Locking arms, they wrestled and rolled and tumbled in the snow, washed each other's faces, flung the snow about—for it was too dry to admit of being wrought into balls—and when tired out, they came back panting and with red cheeks, showing that their lungs had been filled with the life-giving ozone.

It was necessary now and then to cut fuel from the adjacent wood, and this was done by Tim and Jeff. The boys asked to be allowed to try their hand, but they were too unskilful in wielding an axe, and their request was denied. Now and then the howling gale drove the smoke back into the tent, where it was almost as bad as the odor from the pipes.

The four slept at intervals through the day and most of the long night ; but now and then the men laid aside their pipes, the stove "drew," and the atmosphere within was agreeable. The only books in the company were the two pocket Bibles furnished by the mothers of Roswell and Frank. Neither boy forgot his promise to read the volume whenever suitable opportunity presented. Seeing Frank reclining on his blanket, with his little Bible in hand, Jeff asked him to read it aloud, and the boy gladly complied. It was a striking sight, as the men inclined their heads and reverently listened to the impressive words from the Book of Life. There was no jesting or badinage, for that chord which the Creator has placed in every human heart was touched, and responded with sweet music. Many an hour was thus passed—let us hope with profit to every one of the little party.

Finally the longed-for lull in the storm came, and the voyage was renewed. The trip through Caribou Crossing was made without mishap, the distance being about four miles, when they entered Marsh Lake, often known as Mud Lake, though no apparent cause exists for the title. No difficulty was experienced in making their way for the twenty-four miles of its length, at the end of which they debouched into Lynx River, where twenty-seven more miles were passed without incident or trouble worth recording.

CHAPTER X.

" WE'RE doing well," observed Tim McCabe, when the raft with its load and party of gold-seekers reached the end of Lynx River, " but be the same token, we're drawing nigh the worst part of the voyage, and we'll be lucky if we git through the same without mishap."

" What have we ahead ?" asked Jeff.

" Miles Cañon ; it's a little more than half a mile long, and if this raft isn't as strong as it should be it'll be torn to pieces."

Fortunately Jeff had given attention from the first to the stability of the structure, upon which everything depended. He was continually examining it from stem to stern, and where there was a suspicion of the necessity, he drove nails and strengthened the craft in every way possible.

The sail was used whenever possible ; but since they were really among the network of lakes which form the headwaters of the Yukon, the current carried them steadily toward their destination, and there were hours when they scarcely lifted their hands except to keep the raft in proper position by means of the poles. The weather grew steadily milder, for summer was approaching. The snow and ice rapidly melted, and now and then, when the sun shone, the thick clothing felt uncomfortable during the middle of the day. Our friends were in advance of the great multitude that were pushing toward the Klondike from the south, from Canada and to St. Michael's, whence they would start on the two-thousand-mile climb of the Yukon, as soon as it shook off its icy bounds.

It was impossible that the party should not view with solicitude their entrance into Miles Cañon, though Tim assured his friends that much more dangerous rapids would remain to be passed. The cañon is five-eighths of a mile long, with an angry and swift current. Although the raft was tossed about like a cockle-shell, it went through without injury, and none of the goods were displaced or harmed.

Following this came the severest kind of

THE CURRENT WAS NOT ONLY VERY SWIFT, BUT THE CHAN-
NEL WAS FILLED WITH ROCKS.

work. For three miles it seemed as if the river could be no worse, and the raft must be wrenched asunder. The current was not only very swift, but the channel was filled with rocks. Each man grasped one of the strong poles with which the craft was provided, and wrought with might and main to steer clear of the treacherous masses of stone which thrust up their heads everywhere. There were many narrow escapes, and despite the utmost they could do, the raft struck repeatedly. Sometimes it was a bump and sheer to one side so suddenly that the party were almost knocked off their feet. Once, owing to unintentional contrary work the raft banged against the head of a rock and stood still. While the men were desperately plying their poles the current slewed the craft around, and the voyage was resumed.

"Look out!" shouted Jeff; "there's another rock right ahead!"

Unfortunately it was just below the surface, and there were so many ripples and eddies in the current that neither Tim nor Hardman was sure of its exact location, but taking their cue from the leader, they pushed with all their strength to clear the obstruction.

They failed, and the flinty head swept directly under the logs and gouged its course for the entire length of the craft. All felt the jar, and those who could look beneath the upper deck saw the lower timbers rise from the impact, which was so severe that when the raft at last swung free it was barely moving, but, like a wounded horse, it shook itself clear, and the next moment was plunging forward as impetuously as ever. The fears of the party were intensified by sight of wreckage along the banks, proving that more than one of their predecessors had come to grief in trying to make the passage.

While all were on edge with the danger, however, they found themselves at the end of the perilous passage and floating in comparatively smooth water again. Men and boys drew sighs of relief, the former mopping their perspiring brows and looking their mutual congratulations.

"The fun is only just begun," said Tim McCabe; "we had matters purty lively fur a time, but they'll soon be a good deal livelier."

"What is next due?" asked Frank.

"I belave," said Tim, "that some folks

spake of death as riding on a pale horse, don't they?"

" Yes."

" That must be the raison they call the nixt plisure thramp White Horse Cañon, or White Horse Rapids."

" Where are they?"

" But a little way ahid; many men have been drowned in thrying to sail through the same; and him as doesn't know how to swim in a whirlpool hasn't ony business to thry it."

" What, then, do you mean to do?"

" Thry it," was the imperturbable response.

Such talk was not calculated to cheer the listeners, but knowing the Irishman as they did, they received his statement with less serious- ness than they should have done, for he had by no means overrated the peril in their front. Jeff made another examination of the raft while he had the opportunity, and strengthened it in every possible way. He was pleased that it stood the test so well, though it had been se- verely wrenched, and when it crawled over the sunken rock it had narrowly missed being torn asunder. The fastenings of the goods were examined and everything prepared, so far as it could be done, for the crucial trial at hand.

The party were seated in various positions about the raft, looking anxiously ahead, when Tim pointed a little way in advance, with the question :

" Do ye all obsarve that ?"

He indicated a high bank of sand on the right which had been cut out by the erosion of the violent current. Near by some philanthropist had put up a sign, " Keep a Good Look Out."

" You have larned what other people think of the same," he added ; " there's been more than twinty men drowned in there."

" Because they could not swim ?" asked Frank.

" 'Cause the best swimmer in the world can't swim in there ; you and mesilf, boys, will soon be on the same futting, for the raison that we won't have any futting at all."

" How long is the cañon ?"

" Not quite half a mile. Miles Cañon, that we've just passed through, is like a duck-pond alongside the rapids in front of us."

" Can a boat go through ?"

"The thing has been done, but only about one in fifty that starts into them rapids ever raiches the outlet, excipt in bits the size of yer hand."

Frank and Roswell looked at each other in consternation. Was it possible that Jeff would allow the criminal recklessness Tim contemplated? Where the chances were so overwhelmingly against success, it was throwing away their lives to trust themselves to the fearful rapids that had already caused so many deaths.

"If you want to try," said Roswell, excitedly, "you may do so, but neither Frank nor I will. Put us ashore!"

He addressed himself to Jeff, who was seated on the edge of the upper deck, calmly smoking his pipe. He did not look around nor seem to hear the appeal.

"Never mind," interposed Frank; "if they are willing, we are not the ones to back out. I know of no law that prevents a man making a fool of himself."

"Very well," replied his cousin, more composedly, "I am ready."

CHAPTER XI.

JEFF GRAHAM looked inquiringly at Tim
McCabe, who nodded his head by way of reply.
At the same time he said something to Hardman, and all three rose to their feet. Then
the poles were plied with an effect that speedily drove the raft against the bank, where Tim
sprang ashore and secured it. Brave and reckless as was the fellow, he had no intention
of trying to take the boat through the exceed-
ingly dangerous White Horse Rapids, but he
could not refuse the chance for a little amuse-
ment at the expense of his young friends.

In truth, no one should ever attempt to take
a boat through White Horse Rapids. The
best course, perhaps, is to let it drift down the
rapids, guided by a rope one hundred and fifty
feet in length. If it passes through without
material injury, the craft is still at command
below. Another plan is to portage. At this

writing there are roller-ways on the western side, over which the boats can be rolled with a windlass to help pull them to the top of the hill. In lining a craft, it must be done on the right-hand side. Three miles farther down comes the Box Cañon, one hundred yards in length and fifty feet wide, with a chute of terrific velocity. Repeated attempts have been made by reckless miners to take a boat through, but it is much the same as trying to shoot the rapids below Niagara, and the place has well earned its title of "The Miners' Grave." Still, the feat has been performed in safety.

Progress was so effectually barred at White Horse that our friends gave up their raft as of no further use. It was certain to be shattered, and where there was so much timber it was comparatively easy to build another, with which to make the remaining two hundred and twenty miles, particularly as there was no need of constructing a double-decker, for the rough voyaging was at an end.

The goods were, therefore, packed upon the Yukon sleds, and then the raft set adrift. It was never seen again, though an occasional stray log afterward observed bobbing in the current below the rapids may have formed a part of the structure that had served the travellers so well. There was enough snow for the sleds, but the work was exhausting, and was not completed until late in the afternoon, when the tent was set up and camp made.

By the close of the following day the raft was finished. It contained enough pine lumber to float a much heavier load than formed its burden, but, as we have stated, it lacked the double deck, since the necessity for one no longer existed.

The raft was no more than fairly completed when a storm that had been threatening broke upon the party. Since it was expected, and there was no saying how long it would last, the tent was set up and secured in place. Considerable fuel had been gathered, and every preparation was made for a prolonged stay, though it need not be said that each one hoped it would prove otherwise. In a country where for four-fifths of the days the sun does not show itself, such weather must be expected, and, on the whole, our friends counted themselves fortunate that they had been able to make such good progress.

The tent was hardly in position, and all within, huddling around the stove, in which Tim had just started a fire, when they were startled by a hail :

" Halloa, the house !"

The four hurried outside, where a striking sight met them. Eight men, each with a heavy pack strapped over his shoulders, and bending over with his load, thickly clad, but with their faces, so far as they could be seen through the wrappings, wet and red, had halted in front of the tent, which they scrutinized with wonder.

" Are you going to begin digging here ?" called one of the men, whose eyes, nose, and mouth were all that was visible behind his muffler.

" Not while the storm lasts," replied Tim. " If we had room, we'd ask ye to come inside and enj'y yoursilves till the weather clears. At any rate, we'll be glad to give ye something warm to ate and drink."

" Oh, that's it !" exclaimed another of the men. " You're afraid of the storm, are you ?"

" We're not much afraid, but we ain't in love with the same. Won't ye come in—that is, one or two at a time ?"

" Thanks for your invitation, but we haven't the time to spare.   We're afeared they'll get all the gold in the Klondike country if we don't hurry.   You're foolish to loiter along the road like this."

" We're willing to lose a bit of the goold for sake of the comfort.   If ye are bound to go on, we wish ye good luck."

" The same to yourselves," the plucky and hopeful miners called as they plodded forward.

For two dreary days the party was storm-stayed in camp.

" Here," said Jeff Graham, when making ready to resume their voyage, " we leave our Yukon sleds."

" Shall we not need them on our return?" asked Roswell.

" We should if we returned by this route, but I wouldn't work my way against these streams and through the passes again for all the gold in the Klondike country. We shall take the steamer down the Yukon to St. Michael's, and so on to Seattle."

" That is a long voyage," suggested Hard-man.

" Yes, four thousand miles ; but it will be easy enough for us when we are on a steamer."

" The Yukon is closed for eight months or more each year."

" We don't intend to go down it when it's closed, for I didn't bring skates along, and I don't know how to skate, anyway."

" You do not expect to stay long in the Klondike country ?" was the inquiring remark of Hardman, who showed little interest in the intentions of their leader.

" That depends ; we shall come back in two months, or six, or a year, according as to how rich we strike it."

" S'pose you don't strike it at all."

Jeff shrugged his shoulders.

" We'll make a good try for it. If we slip up altogether, these folks I have brought with me won't be any worse off than before ; but I don't intend to slip up—that ain't what I came into this part of the world for."

" No, I reckon few people come for that," was the comment of Hardman, who seemed to be in a cheerful mood again.

Nothing could have offered a stronger contrast to their previous rough experience than that which now came to them. Fourteen miles down the river brought them to Lake Labarge, where they had nothing to do but to sit down and float with the current, using the poles occasionally to keep the raft in the best position. Thirty-one miles brought them to Lewis River, down which they passed to the Hootalinqua; then to the Big Salmon, and forty-five miles farther to the Little Salmon, the current running five miles an hour, and much swifter in the narrow cañon-like passages. Then beyond the Little Salmon the craft and its hopeful passengers floated smoothly with the current for a distance of one hundred and twenty miles, when the boys were startled to see four giant buttes of stone towering above the water, which rushed violently among them.

"What place is that?" asked Frank, who with his cousin surveyed the immense towers with deep interest.

"Five-Finger Rapids," was the reply.

"They look dangerous."

"So they be, unless ye happens to know which two to pass between ; now, which would ye selict as a guess?"

TIM AND JEFF LIT THEIR PIPES; HARDMAN SAT APART.

Roswell and Frank studied them awhile, and the latter answered:

" It doesn't seem to me that it makes much difference which one you take."

" Ah, but it makes a mighty difference. We should have big trouble if we neglicted to folly the right side of the river."

Jeff and Hardman were already working the raft in that direction, and Tim now gave his aid. It looked perilous, but, knowing the right course, the craft made the passage without any mishap. All settled down to enjoy the smooth sailing that was before them once more. Tim and Jeff lit their pipes, Hardman sat apart, while the boys were together near the front of the raft. The weather was clearer than it had been for several days, and much more moderate. May was well advanced, and the short, hot summer was at hand. If all went well, they would reach the gold country at the right season, and as they neared the goal the spirits of all rose, and a longing to get forward manifested itself in many ways. They waited until night had fairly come before they went ashore and encamped, and they were off again at daybreak, despite the uncannily early hour at which it comes in that part of the world.

Six miles down the Lewis River took them to the Rink Rapids, through which they passed without difficulty. Just beyond are the ruins of Fort Selkirk, where the Pelly and Lewis rivers unite. Tim McCabe studied the mouth of the Pelly, as it poured into the Lewis, and soon as the point was fairly passed, he turned to his friends, his round face aglow.

" I offer me congratulations," he said, doffing his cap and bowing low.

" On what ?" asked Frank Mansley.

" The stream over which ye are now floating takes the name of the Yukon, and doesn't give up the same till it tumbles into the Pacific siveral miles to the west of us."

" Several miles !" repeated Frank ; " it must be three thousand."

" Something like that, I belave. The worst part of our journey is behind us."

" How far are we from Juneau ?"

" To be exact, which I loikes to be, it is five hundred and tin miles."

CHAPTER XII.

NATURALLY the route over which the little party of gold-seekers were journeying steadily improved. The Yukon, like many other great rivers of the world, comes into being a lusty, vigorous infant, the junction of the Lewis and Pelly making it a stream of considerable proportions from the moment it takes its name.

Other gold-hunters were seen from time to time, and there were pleasant exchanges and greetings with most of them. It was the custom of Jeff Graham to keep going so long as daylight lasted, when the raft was worked into shore and an encampment made. For a time the old miner kept his Winchester within immediate reach, hoping to gain sight of some deer or wild game, but as day after day and night after night passed without the first glimpse of anything of the kind, he gave up in disgust.

" It's the most villainous country on the face of the earth," he said, as he lit his pipe at the evening fire. " If it wasn't for the gold that we know is here, no decent man would stay over night in it. Frank, tell me something about the confounded country."

" Me !" replied the boy, with a laugh. " I don't know half as much as you and Tim."

" Yes, you do. Tim don't know anything more than the best way to travel through the mountains and across the lakes."

The Irishman took his pipe from between his lips to offer protest against this slur, but changed his mind, and resumed smoking, though his eyes twinkled.

" A man that takes a lot of gold out of the ground and then lets a thief steal it isn't fit to go alone."

" Which is why I've provided mesilf with a chap that knows it all," said Tim, not the least offended, though Hardman scowled, for the remark was a pointed reflection upon him ; but he held his peace.

" What about the Injins here ?" pursued Jeff, addressing the boys ; " they're different from ours in Californy."

Frank had no wish to air his knowledge, but he replied :

" I have read that the natives belong to the red and yellow races—that is, the Indian and Mongolian. There are two stocks of Indians— the Thlinkets and the Tenneh. There are only a few Thlinkets, and they live along the coast. That old Indian who ferried us over Lake Lindeman is a Tenneh, as are the natives of the interior. You may not think they are much like our Indians, but they belong to the Chippewayan family, the same as the Apaches, who have caused so much trouble in Mexico and Arizona."

" That has been my 'pinion," said Tim, who now heard the fact for the first time ; " and the raison why the Alaska redskins ain't as bad as the Apaches is 'cause the weather is so cold it freezes up all the diviltry in them."

" Roswell," continued Jeff, who was proud to show off the learning of his young friends, " why do they call the Eskimos that name ?"

" The name, which means those who eat raw flesh, was given to them by the Indians. They call themselves Aleuts, or Innuits. The Innuits are the same as the Eskimos of Greenland and the Arctic regions, while the Aleuts belong to Alaska, the long, narrow peninsula which extends southwesterly from the mainland and the Aleutian Islands, that look like a continuation of the peninsula.   As for the climate, temperature, and size of Alaska, you and Tim know as much as we do," said Roswell, who disliked as much as his cousin to seem to display his knowledge.

"Why not be modest," gravely asked Tim, "and say that ye knows almost as much as Mr. McCabe, leaving Mr. Graham out of the quistion, be the token that he knows nothing at all, and I'm afeard will niver larn?"

"As you please," replied Roswell; "you and Jeff may settle that between you."

"And ther's nothing to sittle, as me mither used to obsarve whin she looked into the impty coffee-pot; Jiff won't pretind that he knows anything of this country so long as he is in the prisence of mesilf."

"Very true," gravely replied the old miner; "but if I do scoop in any gold, I think I'll know 'nough to shoot any man that tries to steal it."

As he spoke he darted a glance at Hardman,

who was sitting a little back from the fire, also smoking, but glum and silent. The boys wondered why Jeff should make these pointed references, when he had never hinted anything of the kind before, but the old miner had a purpose in mind. While not seeming to pay any special attention to Hardman, he had studied him closely for the past few days, and felt little doubt that he was planning mischief. The words, therefore, that Jeff uttered were meant as a warning to the rogue of what he might expect if he attempted any crooked work.

No further reference was made to the unpleasant subject, although Jeff and Tim chaffed each other for a long time, even after the boys had wrapped themselves in their blankets and lain down to sleep. No watch was set, as would have been the case had they been journeying through a wild part of their own country, for there was nothing to be feared from wild animals or Indians. The only being whom Jeff and the boys distrusted was a member of their own company, and they did not believe he would do anything wrong until after the party had secured something worth the risk on his part.

Deprived of many of the comforts of home and a mother's care, it did not take the boys long, under the tutelage of the older ones, to attend to their own wants. Roswell and Frank soon learned how to sew on a button and do the mending which their garments occasionally required. They washed their clothing and kept themselves in better form than do many men when placed in a similar situation.

With the weather growing more summery and hardly a bit of ice in the river, the raft glided down the Upper Yukon. Ninety-eight miles from the head of the Yukon, the craft passed the mouth of the Milk River, and in this case the party saw the appropriateness of the name, for its water has a perceptible whitish color.

A goodly distance remained to be passed, for it was ten miles to Stewart River, and twenty-five more to Fort Ogilvie, where they spent the night. They were now nearing their journey's end, and all showed a peculiar agitation, such as is natural when we feel ourselves close upon the solution of a problem that has baffled us for a long time.

One form of this emotion was the impatience

AND THE THREE CHEERS WERE GIVEN WITH A WILL.

to get forward faster than before. There was nothing of the feeling when leaving Seattle or Juneau or Dyea, nor did they experience it to any degree while toiling through the hundreds of miles from lake to lake and down the upper waters of the streams which help to form the Yukon.

Roswell and Frank were grateful for one blessed fact—they were stronger and in more rugged health than ever in their lives. When making their way through the passes and helping to drag the sleds, they felt more than once like giving up and turning back, though neither would have confessed it ; but now they were hopeful, buoyant, and eager. They had sent the last letter which they expected to write home for a long time upon leaving Dyea, where they bade good-by to civilization.

The afternoon was young when the raft drifted into a portion of the Yukon which expanded into a width of two miles, where it was joined by another large stream. On the eastern shore loomed a straggling town of considerable proportions.

"Tim," said Frank, suspecting the truth, "what place is that ?"

" Frinds," replied Tim, vainly trying to conceal his agitation, "that town is Dawson City, and the river flowing into ours is the Klondike. Ye have raiched the goold counthry, which, being the same, I rispictfully asks ye all to jine mesilf in letting out a hurrah which will make the town trimble and the payple open their eyes so wide that they won't git them shet agin for a wake to come.   Are ye riddy ? Altogither !"

And the cheers were given with a will.

CHAPTER XIII.

ON THE EDGE OF THE GOLD-FIELDS.

THE little party of gold-seekers had every cause to congratulate themselves, for after a journey of nearly two thousand miles from Seattle, through wild passes, dangerous rapids and cañons, over precipitous mountains, amid storm and tempests, with their lives many a time in peril, half frozen and exhausted by the most wearisome toil, they had arrived at Dawson City, in the midst of the wonderful gold district of the Northwest, all without mishap and in better condition than when they left home.

The boys, in roughing it, had breathed the invigorating ozone and gained in rugged health and strength. Youth and buoyant spirits were on their side, and their muscles, which would have become flabby in the unwholesome atmosphere of a store, were hardened, and their endurance and capacity for trying work immeasurably increased. There are thousands of men to-day enjoying life, without an ache or pain, who owe their splendid condition to the campaigning they underwent in the war for the Union. If that terrific struggle swept multitudes into their graves, it brought the balm of strength and health to many more, who otherwise would not have lived out half their days.

The trying experience of Jeff Graham in his youth and early manhood did this service for him. It was not strange, therefore, that he with his iron muscles bore the strain better than any of his companions. He seemed to be tireless, and his sturdy strength often put others to shame. He had never sapped his constitution by dissipation ; and it may be said that the severe hardships of that journey from Dyea through Chilkoot Pass and the wild regions about the Upper Yukon confirmed that which already existed within his splendid make-up. As for Roswell Palmer and Frank Mansley, their excellent home training, not denying credit to the grim old miner for his wise counsel, had held them free from the bad habits which too often make boys effeminate and weak and old before their time. Gifted by nature with the best of constitutions, they had strengthened rather than undermined them. Neither had known an hour's illness throughout the long, laborious journey, and they were in the best condition possible for the great task that now confronted them.

As for Tim McCabe and Ike Hardman, their weakness lay in yielding to the temptation to drink. No such temptation appeared on the road, and their enforced temperance had the best effect. Tim was less disposed to drink than the other, but, sad to say, he indulged at times. Hardman's ideal was to obtain the means for doing nothing and minister to his base appetites.

It was in 1887 that Dr. George M. Dawson, the leader of an exploring expedition sent by the Canadian Government into the Yukon district, made a report confirming the presence of gold in vast quantities throughout that section. The principal mining camp established there was named in his honor. It faces on one of the banks of the Yukon River, along which it extends for about a mile. It has a sawmill, stores, and churches of the Baptist, Presbyterian, Methodist, and Roman Catholic denominations. Being the headquarters of the Canadian Northwest mounted police, it is one of the best-governed towns on the American continent. At the time of our friends' arrival its population was about four thousand, but the rush will swell it in an incredibly short while to ten, twenty, and possibly fifty times that number, for beyond question it is the centre of the most marvellous gold district that the world has ever known.

Copper, silver, and coal are found in large quantities, but no one gives them a thought when so much of the vastly more attractive yellow metal is within reach. It is singular that while the existence of gold was incontestably known for many years, little or no excitement was produced until 1896 and 1897, when the whole civilized world was turned almost topsy-turvy by the bewildering reports. During the first three months of the latter year more than four million dollars were taken from a space of forty square miles, where a few placer claims were worked. What harvest will be during the next few years no man dare attempt to guess. How suggestive the fact that on one stream so much of the metal has been found that it was given the name " Too Much Gold Creek !"

Inasmuch as our friends are now on the

ground, a few more facts are proper, in order to understand the task that confronted them. Dawson City, it will be remembered, is in British territory, and all the great discoveries of gold have been made to the east of that town. Doubtless gold will be gathered in Alaska itself, but the probabilities are that the richest deposits are upon Canadian soil.

The mining claims begin within two and a half miles of Dawson City, on the Klondike, and follow both sides of that stream into the interior, taking in its tributaries like Hunker's Creek, Gold Bottom, Last Chance, Bear Creek, Bould's Bonanza, and El Dorado. Of these the richest are El Dorado, Gold Bottom, Hunker, and the oddly named Too Much Gold Creek. The last is the farthest from Dawson City, and the least known ; but there can be no question that numerous other streams, at present unvisited, are equally rich, and will be speedily developed.

Just now placer mining is the only method employed. According to the mining laws of the Northwest, the words " mine," " placer mine," and " diggings" mean the same thing, and refer to any natural stratum or bed of earth, gravel, or cement mined for gold or other precious mineral. There is very little quartz mining, or crushing of rocks, as is practised in many sections of California. This requires expensive machinery, and little necessity for it seems to exist in the Klondike. In placer mining the pay dirt is washed by the simplest methods, such as were practised in California during the pioneer days.

Everything was hurry and bustle at Dawson City on that day, late in May, when our friends arrived. It was a noticeable fact that the date of their arrival was exactly two months after the boys kissed their parents good-by in San Francisco.

Tim McCabe had gathered much practical knowledge during his experience in this region, while Jeff had not forgotten what he passed through " in the days of '49," to which wisdom he had added, as opportunity presented, while on the way to the Klondike. When the party had eaten together at the principal hotel and the men had lit their pipes in a group by themselves, a surprise came. The old miner smoked a minute or two in silence, and then turned to Hardman, who was sitting a little apart, moody and reserved.

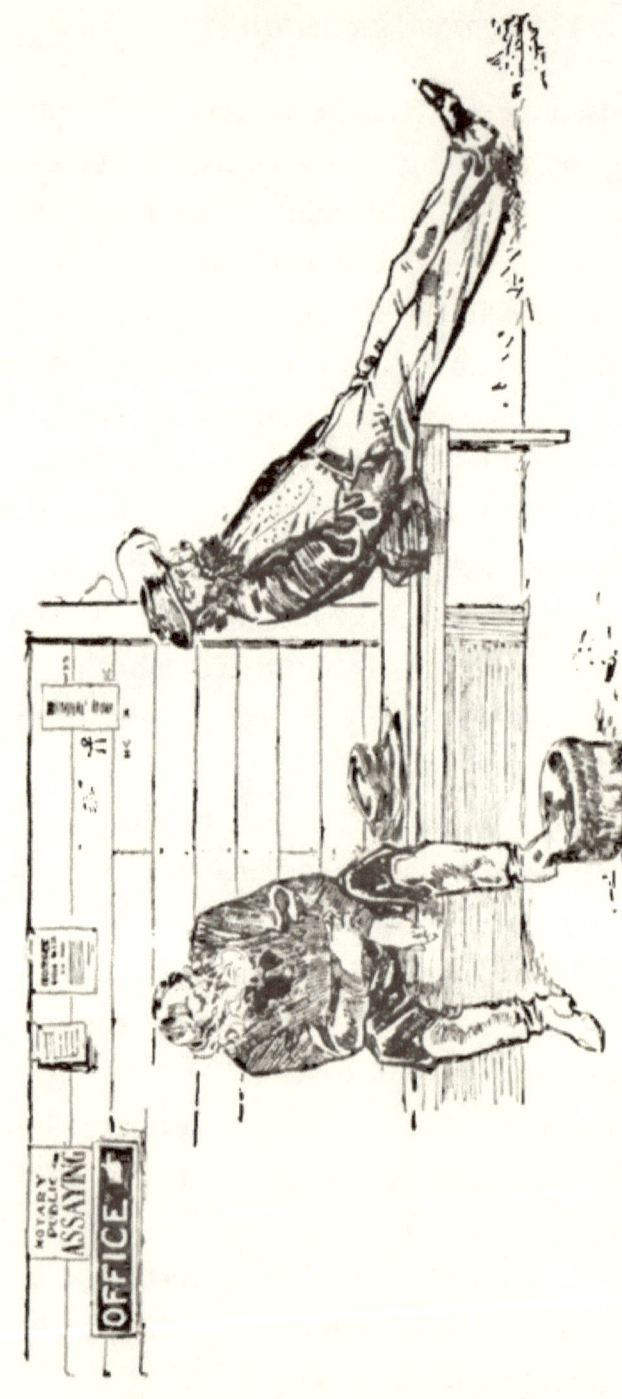

"I DON'T SEE THE USE OF YOUR HARPING ON THAT AFFAIR," SAID HARDMAN.

" Ike," said he, " I've stood by you all the way from Juneau, hain't I ?"

The fellow looked wonderingly at him, as did the others, none suspecting what was coming.

" In course," was the gruff reply of Hardman ; " we all stood by one another, fur if we hadn't we wouldn't stood at all."

" You've got to Dawson City without it costing you a penny, haven't you ?"

" There hain't been much chance to spend money since we left Dyea," replied Hardman with a grin.

Jeff was nettled by this dodging of the issue ; but he kept his temper.

" And if there had been you hadn't a dollar to spend onless you kept back some of that which you stole from Tim."

" I don't see the use of your harping on that affair," said Hardman angrily. " I've owned up, and am going to make it all right with Tim. It's none of your business, anyway, and I don't want to hear any more of it."

" Well, what I'm getting at is this : if it hadn't been for me you'd never got to this place. You're here, and now you must look out for yourself ; I won't have you an hour

longer in the party ; we part ; get away as
soon as you can !"

Hardman looked savagely at the old miner,
as if suspecting he had not heard aright. But
a moment's reflection convinced him there was
no mistake. With a muttered imprecation he
rose to his feet and left. But it was by no
means the last of him.

CHAPTER XIV.

PROSPECTING.

AFTER the departure of Hardman, Jeff explained to Tim why he had driven him from their company. He told what Frank had seen when crossing Lake Lindeman, and how the fellow afterward, when he thought all were asleep within the tent, went out to meet his confederate.

" I didn't want to turn him loose on the road," added Jeff, " though I had half a mind to tell him to hunt up his friends and join them. But he now has the same chance as the rest of us, and must look out for himself."

" Begorra, but ye are right, Jiff," was the hearty response of the Irishman. " I'm beginning to suspict that he didn't intind to give back that money he borrered—that is, if he should iver lay hands on the same."

Jeff looked pityingly at his friend ; but reading in the expression of his face that he was jesting, he made no response. Instead, he spoke impressively :

" You never would have lost that money if you hadn't been in liquor."

" That's the fact, Jiff ; but how did ye find it out ?"

" My own common sense told me. You've been looking 'round the last hour for a chance to indulge agin."

" I'll admit," was the frank response, " that a dim idea of the kind has been flickerin' through me brain ; but I cast the timptation indignantly behind me. Do you know why ?"

" No."

" Nobody offered to pay for the drinks, and I haven't a cint to pay for any mesilf."

" And you won't get a cent from me ; you must earn it by taking out gold. If you succeed it'll be yours, and you can do as you please with it."

Tim removed his cap and scratched his head.

" I've gone a good many wakes without it, and I feel so much better that I'm thinking of keeping up the good work."

" I hope you will, and prove yourself a man

of sense. But we have no time to waste ; we oughter be on our way now."

The sentiment suited all, and was followed without delay. Amid the crush and hustle it was impossible to hire a horse, mule, donkey, or boat. Everything had been engaged long before, and there were hundreds of disappointed applicants who, like our friends, were obliged to make the tramp eastward on foot, carrying their utensils with them, and leaving behind all that was not necessary in the work of placer mining.

During the brief stay at Dawson City the four attentively studied such maps as they could secure, and gathered all information from the many who were qualified and willing to give it. As a consequence, when they started up the Klondike, they had a well-defined idea of their destination.

The first stream which flows into the river from the southward is the Bonanza, some twenty-five miles long. This itself has numerous small tributaries emptying into it ; but hearing that all claims had been located, and not believing it possible that any valuable ones had been overlooked, they pushed on to Twelve

Mile Creek, also flowing from the south. There the same facts confronted them, and camping on the road when necessary, our friends finally reached Too Much Gold Creek, thirty-five miles from Dawson.

Gold-hunters were all around them, and frequently the men and boys tramped for miles in the company of men whom they had never seen before ; but such a life levels social distinctions, and they were soon upon as friendly terms as if they had come from Seattle in company.

At the mouth of Too Much Gold Creek they encountered two grizzly miners, each mounted on a mule that was so covered with additional luggage that little besides his head, ears, and forefeet was visible. They intended to cross the Klondike and prospect on the other side. Jeff asked whether there was no gold along the creek which they had just descended.

" It's full of it," was the reply of the elder ; " but we're too late ; all the claims have been taken up."

" Did you go to the headwaters ?"

" No ; we didn't want to waste the time, when all the claims are gone ; there are other places as good as that, and we'll strike one; so good-by, friends."

Laughing and in high spirits, the two miners struck their boot heels against the ribs of their mules and were off. It may be worth recording that both of them struck it rich within the following week, and a month later started for home rich men.

"It ain't likely," said Jeff, "that there are many claims left along this river; but there must be some. Anyhow, we'll try it; I'm sure there are places among those mountains that nobody has visited."

To the east and south towered a spur of the Rocky Mountains. It would take hundreds of men a long time thoroughly to explore their recesses, and it was the intention of the leader to push in among them. The region resembled that to which he had been accustomed in California, and he would feel more at home there.

So the wearisome tramp was resumed and continued, with occasional rests, until late at night. Other parties were continually encountered, and all had the same story to tell of there not being a foot of desirable land that was not pre-empted. Some of these people were returning, but most of them pressed on, hopeful of striking some spot that was awaiting them.

Encamping under the shelter of a rock, the journey was resumed early the next morning, and, some twenty miles from the Klondike, a turn was made eastward among the mountains, which stretch far beyond the farthest range of vision. They were following a small stream that showed no signs of having been visited, and by noon had reached a point where they seemed as much alone as if in the depths of Africa.

" I guess we may as well try it here," said Jeff, and he began to unload his pack, in which he was promptly imitated by his companions. They quickly finished, and sat down for a long rest.

It had been a steady climb almost from the first. But for their previous severe training the boys would have succumbed, but they stood it well. The stream which flowed in front of them was little more than a brook, that seemed to be made by the melting snows above. It was clear and cold, and they drank deeply from it. Rocks and bowlders were above, below, in front, and at the rear.

When their utensils and equipage were laid in a pile, Jeff went off in one direction, Tim in another, while the boys plunged deeper into the mountains, all engaged in prospecting as best they could. Inasmuch as the boys had never had any experience in that sort of work, their only chance of success was through accident.

They followed up the stream, as nearly as they could judge, for about an eighth of a mile, still among the huge rocks, when they sat down to rest.

" We may as well go back," cried Roswell, " for Jeff and Tim are the only ones who know when they have come upon signs of gold ; we may have passed a half-dozen places where it can be taken out by the bushel—"

Frank touched his cousin's arm and indicated by a nod of his head a pile of rocks a few rods away and a short distance above them. Looking thither, they saw the head and shoulders of a man intently studying them. When he found he was observed he lowered his head and disappeared.

" Do you know him ?" asked Frank, in an undertone.

" No ; I never saw him before."

" Yes, you have. He crossed Lake Lindeman with us. He's the one that signalled to Hardman and afterward met him at night outside of our tent."

CHAPTER XV.

A FIND.

It was an unpleasant discovery to the boys that after parting company with the ill-favored man who was known to be a friend and comrade of the rogue Ike Hardman, and after travelling hundreds of miles to this lonely spot, they should meet the fellow again. Doubtless he was engaged on the same errand as themselves, and the presumption was that sooner or later he would be joined by Hardman.

" I don't know that there is any danger," said Roswell ; " but it would be more comfort- able to know they were not going to be our neighbors."

" Let's follow up the man and question him," said Frank, starting to climb the rocks behind which the other's face had vanished. It took only a few minutes to reach the spot ; but when they did so, and looked around, nothing was seen of him.

" He evidently doesn't wish to make our acquaintance," said Frank.

" I hope he will continue to feel that way; we must tell Jeff and Tim about this. Let's hurry back to camp."

They now started to descend the stream, which they had followed from the point where they left their luggage. By using the brook as their guide, they were in no danger of losing their way.

About half the distance was passed when they came to a point where the walking looked better on the other side. The stream was so narrow that Frank, who was in the lead, easily leaped across. Roswell started to follow, but tripped and fell on his hands and knees, one foot splashing in the water, which was only a few inches in depth and as clear as crystal.

" Are you hurt ?" asked Frank, pausing and looking around at him.

" Not a bit. I don't know what made me so awkward."

" Halloa ! what's that ?"

At first Frank thought it was a small fish holding itself stationary in the brook ; but that could not be, and he stooped down to see more

"IT'S GOLD!" HE EXCLAIMED.

clearly. With an exclamation, he dashed his
hand into the water and drew out a rough,
irregular nugget nearly two inches in diameter
each way. It was bright yellow in color, and
so heavy that there could be no doubt of its
nature.

" It's gold !" he exclaimed in a half-fright-
ened undertone, as he passed it to Roswell, who
was as much excited as he. He " hefted" it
and held it up to the light.

" No mistake, it is. I wonder what it is
worth."

" Several hundred dollars at least. I'll bet
there are lots more about here."

They straightway began a vigorous search
up and down stream, confident of finding other
similar nuggets, but none was discovered, and
finally they reached the place where their baggage had been left, and where Tim and Jeff
were awaiting them.

" Look !" called the delighted Frank, holding up the nugget. " See what we found !"

" Begorra, but I shouldn't wonder if that's
worth something," remarked Tim, catching the
contagion. Jeff merely smiled and reached out
his hand without any appearance of excitement.

" Let me have a look at it."

He never used glasses, nor did he bring any acid with which to test such yellow metals as they might find, for he needed neither. He had been trained too well in his early manhood.

The instant he noted its great weight he was convinced of the truth. But, without speaking for a minute or two, he turned the nugget over, held it up to the light, and then put it between his big, sound teeth as if it were a hickory-nut which he wished to crack. He looked at the abrasion made by his teeth, tossed the nugget several feet in the air, and, catching it in his palm as it descended, said :

" That's pure gold. Haven't you any more ?"

" No," replied Frank ; " we searched, but couldn't find any."

Jeff moved his hand up and down and closed one eye, as if that would help him to estimate the weight more exactly.

" I should say that it is worth from six to eight hundred dollars : you younkers have made purty good wages for to-day. I hope," he added quizzically, " you'll be able to keep it up."

" And how have you made out ?" asked Roswell.

" Tim says he didn't come onto anything that looks like pay dirt ; but I struck a spot that gives me hope. We'll locate here for a while."

Of course it was impossible for the party to bring any material with them from which to construct a dwelling. The regulation miner's cabin is twelve by fourteen feet, with walls six or seven feet high, and gables two feet higher. It consists of a single room, with the roof heavily earthed and the worst sort of ventilation, owing to the small windows and the necessity of keeping warm in a climate that sometimes drops to fifty or sixty degrees below zero. The miners keep close within the cabins during the terrible winter weather, or, if it permits, they sink a shaft to bed-rock and then tunnel in different directions. The ground never thaws below a depth of two feet, so there is no need of shoring to prevent its caving. The pay dirt is brought up by means of a small windlass and thrown into a heap, where it remains until spring, when it is washed out.

Since the season was well advanced, the

men and boys prepared themselves to wash the pay dirt whenever found. But, first of all, it was necessary to establish a home for themselves while they remained in the region. They had a single axe and a few utensils besides the shovels, pans, and articles required in their work. While Tim was prospecting, he gave more attention to searching for a site for a home than for gold, and was fortunate enough to find a place among the rocks, which was fitted up quite comfortably. The stone furnished three and a part of four walls necessary, and they cut branches, which were spread over the top and covered with dirt for the roof. Owing to the moderate weather and the trouble from smoke, the fire was kindled on the outside when required for cooking purposes. The Yukon stove, because of its weight, was left at Dawson City, whither one of them expected to go when it became necessary to replenish their stores. Although the nights were still cold, the weather was comparatively comfortable. Before long it would become oppressive during the middle of the day.

As Jeff figured it out, they had enough food, tobacco, and supplies to last for a couple of weeks, or possibly longer. If they struck a claim which they wished to stake out, it would be necessary for one of them to go to Dawson City to register it, the process being quite simple.

The prospector is forbidden to exceed five hundred feet up and down a stream, following the course of the valley, but the width may run from base to base of the mountains. Thus a miner's claim is one of the few things that is often broader than it is long. Should the stream have no other claims located upon it, the one thus made is known as the " the discovery claim," and the stakes used are marked 0. This claim is the starting-point, the next one up and the next down the stream being marked No. 1, and there can be only two such on any stream.

Next, four stakes must be driven in place, each being marked with the owner's initials and the letters " M. L.," meaning " mining location," after which it must be bounded with cross or end lines, and within the ensuing sixty days the claim has to be filed with the government's recorder at Dawson City. Should a claim be staked before the discovery of gold, the prospector has sixty days in which to find the metal.   If he fails to do so in the time mentioned, his claim lapses, since it is absolutely essential that he shall find gold in order to hold it permanently.

CHAPTER XVI.

THE CLAIM.

NOT the least interesting feature of the stay of our friends in the gold region was their dwelling during those memorable days. The rocks came so nearly together that an irregular open space was left, which averaged a width of twenty feet with a depth slightly less. Thus three sides and the floor were composed of solid stone. When the roof, as described, was put in place, the dwelling had the appearance of a cavern fully open at the front. There the canvas composing the tent was stretched, and so arranged that the dwelling, as it may be called, was completed. It was inclosed on all sides, with the door composed of the flaps of the tent, which could be lowered at night, so that the inmates were effectually protected against the weather, though had there been any prowling wild animals or intruding white men near, they would have had little difficulty in forcing an entrance. It has been explained how all trouble from the smoke of a fire was avoided.

One of the peculiarities of this primitive house was its interior arrangement. There were so many projecting points on the walls that they were utilized as pegs upon which to hang the extra garments. A ledge a couple of feet above the floor served as a couch, upon which the boys spread their blankets, while the men laid theirs on the floor itself. The mining and cooking utensils were neatly arranged against the rear wall, where were piled the small canvas bags intended to contain the gold dust and nuggets that were to be gathered.

Jeff expressed the truth when he said :

" This will sarve us well while the weather is moderate ; but if we should be here when the thermometer goes down to fifty or sixty degrees below zero, we'd turn into icicles before we could say Jack Robinson."

Hardly pausing to place their house in order, the party set out to investigate the find which Jeff hoped he had made.

Going up the stream for a short distance, they turned off into a narrow valley, which never would have attracted the attention of the boys.

The old miner stood for some minutes attentively studying his surroundings, and then, instead of beginning to dig, as his companions expected him to do, he said with an expression of disgust :

" Boys, I've made a mistake ; there's no gold here."

" How can you tell until you search ?" asked the astonished Roswell.

" It ain't what I thought it was ; you don't find the stuff in places like this. There's no use of wasting time ; come on."

Wondering at his action, the three, smiling but silent, trailed after him. Climbing over some intervening bowlders, they shortly emerged into a place altogether different from any they had yet seen. It was a valley two or three hundred feet in width, with the sides gently sloping. There was no snow on the ground, and here and there a few green blades of grass could be seen sprouting from the fertile soil. Through the middle of this valley meandered a stream eight or ten feet in width, but shallow, and so clear that the bottom could be plainly

seen while yet some distance away. The val
ley itself soon curved out of sight above, and it
was impossible, therefore, to guess its extent
in that direction. Below it terminated, not far
from where they stood, the rocks coming together so as to form a small cañon, through
which the creek rushed with a velocity that
reminded them of the dangerous ones they had
passed on their way from Chilkoot Pass.

"Wait here a bit," said Jeff, as he started
toward the stream. The others obeyed, watching his actions with interest.

He strode to the creek, along which he
walked a few rods, his head bent as he carefully scrutinized all that passed under his eye.
Suddenly he stopped and stared as if he had
found that for which he was looking. Then
stooping down, he leaned as far out as he could,
gathered a handful of the gravelly soil, and
put it in the washer which he had taken with
him. This was repeated several times. Then
he dipped the pan so as nearly to fill it with
water, after which he whirled it round several
times with a speed that caused some of the
water to fly out. That part of his work completed, he set down the pan which served as a

washer, and walked rapidly back toward his friends.

" Another disappointment," remarked Frank ; " it isn't as easy to find gold as we thought."

" I don't know about that," said Tim McCabe. " Jiff looks to me as if he has hit on something worth while. How is it, Jiff?" he called as the old miner drew near.

" That's our claim," he replied ; " we'll stake it out, and then I'm going to Dawson to file it."

" Are you sure there is gold here ?" asked Roswell, in some excitement.

" Yes, I hit it this time. We mustn't lose any days in staking it out, or somebody else will get ahead of us."

The assurance of Jeff imparted confidence to the rest. The stakes were cut and driven, according to the rule already stated, and then Jeff breathed more freely.

" We've got sixty days to find the stuff," he said, " and nobody daren't say a word to us. All the same, I'm going to Dawson to file the claim and make things dead sure."

" When will you go ?"

" Now, right off. I want to bring back

some things with me, and I'll be gone two or three days, but I won't lose no time."

Jeff was one of those men who do not require long to make up their minds, and whom, having reached a decision, nothing can turn aside from its execution. Ten minutes later he was hurrying toward Dawson City, forty miles or more distant.

Inasmuch as Tim McCabe had practical knowledge of placer mining, the three decided to improve the time while Jeff was absent in taking out some of the gold which he assured them was there.

As has been explained, this form of mining is of the crudest and cheapest nature. In winter, after sinking a shaft to bed-rock, tunnels are run in different directions, and the frozen dirt piled up until warm weather permits its washing out. The distance to bed-rock varies from four to twenty feet. The gold is found in dust, grains, and nuggets, the last varying from the size of a hickory-nut or larger to small grains of pure gold.

It quite often occurs that the bed-rock is seamy, with many small depressions. It is supposed that when the *débris* containing the orig-

THE BOYS STOOD ATTENTIVELY WATCHING THE OPERATION.

inal gold swept over this bed-rock, the great weight of the metal caused it to fall and lodge in the crevices, where it has lain for ages. Certain it is that the richest finds have been made in such places.

Having fixed upon the spot where the work should begin, Tim McCabe and the boys set to work to clear off the coarse gravel and stone from a patch of ground. At the end of several hours they had completed enough to begin operations. Tim dropped a few handfuls of the finer gravel or sand into his pan, which was a broad, shallow dish of sheet iron. Then water was dipped into the pan until it was full, when he whirled it swiftly about and up and down. This allowed the gold, on account of its greater specific gravity, to fall to the bottom, while the sand itself was floated off by the agitation. Tim had learned the knack of dipping the pan sideways, so as gradually to get rid of the worthless stuff, while the heavy yellow particles remained below.

The boys stood attentively watching the operation, which was carried on with such skill that by and by nothing was left in the bottom but the yellow and black particles. The latter were pulverized magnetic iron ore, which almost always accompanies the gold. Frank's and Roswell's eyes sparkled as they saw so much of the yellow particles, even though it looked almost as fine as the black sand.

"How will you separate them?" asked Frank.

"Now ye'll observe the use that that cask is to be put to," replied Tim, "if ye'll oblige me by filling the same with water."

This was done, when Tim flung about a pound of mercury into the cask, after which he dumped into it the black and yellow sand. As soon as the gold came in contact with the mercury it formed an amalgam.

"This will do to start things," said Tim. "When we have enough to make it pay, we'll squaze it through a buckskin bag."

"What is the result?"

"Nearly all the mercury will ooze through the bag, and we can use the same agin in the cask. The impure goold will be placed on a shovel and held over a hot fire till the mercury has gone off in vapor, and only the pure goold is lift, or rather there's just a wee bit of the mercury still hanging 'bout the goold; but we'll make a big improvement whin Jiff comes back. The filing of this claim ain't the only thing that takes him to Dawson City."

" What do you think of the deposit here ?"

" I b'lave it's one of the richest finds in the Kloondike counthry, and if it turns out as it promises, we shall go home and live like gintlemen the rist of our lives."

CHAPTER XVII

TIM McCABE and the boys wrought steadily through the rest of the day and the following two days. Inasmuch as the summer sun in the Klondike region does not thaw the soil to a greater depth than two feet, it was necessary to pile wood upon the earth and set it afire. As this gradually dissolved the frozen ground, the refuse dirt was cleared away, so as to reach paying earth or gravel. The results for a time were disappointing. The gold-hunters secured a good deal of yellow grains or dust, and ordinarily would have been satisfied, but naturally they were greedy for more.

There came times of discouragement, when the boys began to doubt the truth of the wonderful stories that had reached them from the Klondike region, or they thought that if perchance the reports were true, they themselves and their friends had not hit upon a productive spot. Tim, when appealed to, had little to say, but it was of a hopeful nature. It would have been unnatural had he not been absorbed in the work in hand.

That there was gold was undeniable, for the evidence was continually before them, but the question was whether it was to be found in paying quantities upon their claim. At the close of the second day all they had gathered was not worth ten dollars.

But the harvest rewarded them on the third day. Tim was working hard and silently, when he suddenly leaped to his feet, flung down his pick, and hurling his cap in the air, began dancing a jig and singing an Irish ditty. The boys looked at him in amazement, wondering whether he had bidden good-by to his senses.

"Do ye observe that beauty?" he asked, stopping short and holding up a yellow nugget as large as the one the boys had taken from the brook several days before. Roswell and Frank hurried up to him and examined the prize. There could be no doubt that it was virgin gold and worth several hundred dollars.

Twenty minutes later it was Roswell's turn to hurrah, for he came upon one almost as large.   And he did hurrah, too, and his friends joined in with a vigor that could not be criticised.   Congratulating one another, the three paused but a few minutes to inspect the finds, when they were digging harder than ever.

" I think it is my turn," remarked Frank ; " you fellows are becoming so proud, that if I don't find—by George, *I have found it !*"

Incredible as it seemed, it was true, and Frank's prize was larger than any of the others.   Instantly they were at work again, glowing with hope and delight.   No more nuggets were taken out that day, but the gravel revealed greater richness than at any time before.

Jeff Graham put in an appearance while they were eating supper, and, to the surprise of all, he was riding a tough little burro, which he had bought at Dawson for five hundred dollars.   His eyes sparkled when he learned what had been done during his absence, but he quietly remarked, " I knowed it," and having turned his animal loose, after unloading him, he asked for the particulars.

Although it was quite cold, the four remained seated on the bowlders outside of their primitive dwelling, the men smoking their pipes and discussing the wonderful success they had had, and the still greater that was fairly within their grasp.

" We're not so much alone as I thought," remarked Jeff, " for there are fifty miners to the east and north, and some of them ain't far from where we've staked out our claim, and more are coming."

" They can't interfere with us ?" was the inquiring remark of Roswell.

" Not much. As a rule, folks don't file their claims till they've struck onto a spot where the yaller stuff shows; but I've done both, 'cause I was sartin that we'd hit it rich. If anybody tried to jump our claim, the first thing I'd do would be to shoot him ; then I'd turn him over to the mounted police that are looking after things all through this country."

" Ye mane that ye'd turn over what was lift of his remains," suggested Tim gravely.

" It would amount to that. Things are in better shape here than they was in the old times in Californy, where a man had to fight for what he had, and then he wasn't always able to keep it."

" What do you intend to do with the burro ?" asked Frank.

" Let him run loose till we need him. He brought a purty good load of such things as we want, and I'm hoping he'll have another kind of load to take back," was the significant reply of the old miner.

This was the nearest Jeff came to particulars. His natural reserve as to what he had done and concerning his plans for the future prevented any further enlightenment. The fact that they had neighbors at no great distance was both pleasing and displeasing. Despite the assurance of their leader, there was some misgiving that when the richness of the find became known an attempt would be made to rob them. Gold will incite many men to commit any crime, and with the vast recesses of the Rocky Mountain spur behind them, the criminals might be ready to take desperate chances.

It was hardly light the next morning when the party were at it again. The pan or hand method of washing the gold is so slow and laborious that with the help and superintendence of Jeff a " rocker" was set up. This was a box about three feet long and two wide, made in two parts. The upper part was shallow, with a strong sheet-iron bottom perforated with quarter-inch holes. In the middle of the other part of the box was an inclined shelf, which sloped downward for six or eight inches at the lower end. Over this was placed a piece of heavy woollen blanket, the whole being mounted upon two rockers, like those of an ordinary child's cradle. These were rested on two strong blocks of wood to permit of their being rocked readily.

This device was placed beside the running stream. As the pay dirt was shovelled into the upper shallow box, one of the party rocked it with one hand while with the other he ladled water. The fine particles with the gold fell through the holes upon the blanket, which held the gold, while the sand and other matter glided over it to the bottom of the box, which was so inclined that what passed through was washed down and finally out of the box. Thin slats were fixed across the bottom of the box, with mercury behind them, to catch such particles of gold as escaped the blanket.

The stuff dug up by our friends was so nuggety that many lumps remained in the upper box, where they were detained by their weight, while the lighter stuff passed through, and the smaller lumps were held by a deeper slat at the further end of the bottom of the box. When the blanket became surcharged with wealth it was removed and rinsed in a barrel of water, the particles amalgamating with the mercury in the bottom of the barrel.

Sluicing requires plenty of running water with considerable fall, and is two or three times as rapid as the method just described, but since it was not adopted by our friends, a description need not be given.

At the end of a week Jeff, with the help of his companions, made a careful estimate of the nuggets and sand which they had gathered and stowed away in the cavern where they slept and took their meals. As nearly as they could figure it out the gold which they had collected was worth not quite one hundred thousand dollars—very fair wages, it will be conceded, for six days' work by two men and two boys. On Sunday they conscientiously abstained from labor, though it can hardly be said that their thoughts were elsewhere.

Since one hundred thousand dollars in gold

weighs in the neighborhood of four hundred pounds, it will be seen that the party had already accumulated a good load to be distributed among themselves. It may have been that the expectation of this result caused Jeff to bring the burro back, for with his help it would not be hard to carry double the amount, especially as everything else would be left behind.

To the surprise of his friends, Jeff announced that it was necessary for him to make another visit to Dawson City. It was important business that called him thither, but he gave no hint of its nature. He hoped to be back within two or three days, and he departed on foot, leaving the animal to recuperate, and, as he grimly added, "make himself strong enough to carry a good load to town."

Jeff left early in the morning. The afternoon was about half gone, when Tim with an expression of anxious concern announced that he had just remembered something which required him to go to Dawson without an hour's delay.

" It's queer that I didn't think of the same while Jiff was here," he said, " so that he might have enj'yed the plisure of me society, but it won't be hard for me to find him after I git there.   Ye byes wont be scared of being lift to yersilves fur a few days?" he asked with so much earnestness that they hastened to assure him he need have no misgivings on that point.

" We shall keep hard at it while you are away, but since Jeff is also absent we shall be lonely."

" Luk fur me very soon.   I'll advise Jiff to make ye an extra allowance for yer wurruk while him and me is doing nothing."

Two hours after the departure of McCabe, Frank, who was working the rocker while his chum was shovelling in the dirt, suddenly stopped, with expanding eyes.

" I have just thought what Tim's business is at Dawson."

" What is it?"

" It is his longing for drink.   He has gone on a spree, taking one of his nuggets with him to pay the cost.   Jeff will be sure to run across him, and then there will be music."

"I HAVE JUST THOUGHT WHAT TIM'S BUSINESS IS AT DAWSON," SAID FRANK.

CHAPTER XVIII.

A STARTLING DISCOVERY.

THE weather was mild, for the short, oppressive Northwest summer was rapidly approaching. During the middle of the day the sun was hot, and the boys perspired freely. By and by would come the billions of mosquitoes to render life unbearable. Those pests often kill bears and wolves by blinding them, and the man who does not wear some protection is driven frantic, unable to eat, sleep, or live, except in smothering smoke. Jeff had said that he meant to complete the work, if possible, and start down the Yukon before that time of torment arrived.

For two days the boys wrought incessantly. They had learned how to wash and purify the gold in the crude way taught them by the old miner, and the rich reward for their labor continued. Jeff had brought back on his previous visit to Dawson City an abundant supply of strong canvas bags, in which the gold was placed, with the tops securely tied. These were regularly deposited in the cavern where the party made their home, until a row of them lined one side of the place. It was a striking proof of the wonderful richness of their find, that one of these bags was filled wholly with nuggets, which must have been worth fifteen or twenty thousand dollars.

Early on the afternoon of the third day another thought struck Frank Mansley, and he ceased shovelling gravel into the rocker for his companion.

"What is it now?" asked Roswell with a smile.

"Don't you remember that on the first day we arrived here, while we were prospecting up the little stream, we saw that friend of Ike Hardman?"

"Yes, of course."

"Well, we never told Jeff about it."

"I declare!" exclaimed Roswell. "How came we to forget it?"

"This gold drove it out of our minds. I never thought of it until this minute. I tell you, Roswell, I believe something has gone wrong."

And Frank sat down, removed his cap, and wiped his moist forehead with his handker·chief.

" What could have gone wrong ?" asked the other lad, who, despite his jauntiness, shared in a degree the anxiety of his friend.

" All the gold we have gathered is in the cavern. I believe Hardman and those fellows are in the neighborhood and mean to steal it."

" It's a pity we didn't think of this before," said Roswell, laying down his shovel. " Let's go back to the cavern and keep watch till Jeff comes back."

Inspired by their new dread, they hastily gathered up what gold had been washed out, stowed it into another canvas bag, and then Frank slung it half filled over his shoulder and started for the cavern, something more than an eighth of a mile away.

They walked fast and in silence, for the thought in the mind of both was the same. From the first the most imprudent carelessness had been shown, and they could not understand how Jeff ever allowed the valuable store to re-main unguarded. It is true, as has already been stated, that the section, despite the rush of lawless characters that have flocked thither, is one of the best governed in the world, and no officers could be more watchful and effective than the mounted police of the Northwest; but the course of our friends had much the appearance of a man leaving his pocketbook in the middle of the street and expecting to find it again the next day.

A bitter reflection of the boys was that this never would have been the case had they told Jeff of the presence of the suspicious individual in the neighborhood. If anything went amiss, they felt that the blame must rest with them If matters were found right, they would not leave the cavern until one or both of their friends returned.

When half the distance was passed, Roswell, who was in the lead, broke into a lope, with Frank instantly doing the same. A minute later they had to slacken their pace because of the need to climb some bowlders and make their way through an avenue between massive rocks, but the instant it was possible they were trotting again.

It had been the custom for the gold-seekers to take a lunch with them to the diggings.

"WE HAVE BEEN ROBBED! ALL THE GOLD IS GONE."

This saved time, and their real meal was eaten in the evening after their return home.

The moment Roswell caught sight of the round, irregular opening which served as the door of their dwelling, he anxiously scanned it and the pile of wood and embers on the outside, where the fire was kindled for cooking purposes. The fact that he saw nothing amiss gave him hope, but did not remove the singular distrust that had brought both in such haste from the diggings.

He ran faster, while Frank, discommoded by the heavy, bouncing bag over his shoulder, stumbled, and his hat fell off. With an impatient exclamation he caught it up, recovered himself, and was off again.

As he looked ahead he saw Roswell duck his head and plunge through the opening.

"Is everything right?" shouted Frank, whose dread intensified with each passing second.

Before he could reach the door out came his cousin, as if fired by a catapult. His eyes were staring and his face as white as death.

"Right!" he gasped; "we have been robbed! All the gold is gone!"

And overcome by the shock the poor fellow collapsed and sank to the ground as weak as a kitten. Frank let the bag fall and straightened up.

"No : it cannot be," he said in a husky voice.

" Look for yourself," replied Roswell, swallowing a lump in his throat and turning his eyes pitifully toward his comrade.

A strange fear held Frank motionless for several seconds. Despite the startling declaration of his cousin, a faint hope thrilled him that he was mistaken, and yet he dared not peer into the interior through dread of finding he was not.

Reflecting, however, upon the childish part he was playing, he pulled himself together, and with the deliberation of Jeff Graham himself bent his head and passed through the door.

Enough sunlight penetrated the cavern to reveal the whole interior in the faint illumination. When they left that morning the row of canvas bags was neatly arranged along the farther wall, where they stood like so many corpulent little brownies.

Every one had vanished.

Frank Mansley stared for a moment in silence. Then he stepped forward and called in a strong, firm voice :

" Come, Roswell, quick !"

The other roused himself and hastily advanced.

" Take your revolver," said Frank, as he shoved his own into his hip-pocket, and begun strapping Jeff's cartridge belt around his waist. As Roswell obeyed, his cousin took the Winchester from where it leaned in one corner.

" Now for those thieves, and we don't come back till we find them."

CHAPTER XIX.

THE TRAIL INTO THE MOUNTAINS.

On the outside of the cavern the boys halted. After the shock both were comparatively calm. Their faces were pale, and they compressed their lips with resolution. Some time during the preceding few hours thieves had entered their home and carried away one hundred thousand dollars in gold dust and nuggets, and the youths were determined to regain the property, no matter what danger had to be confronted.

But the common sense of the boys told them the surest way to defeat their resolve was to rush off blindly, with not one chance in a thousand of taking the right course.

"Roswell, that gold weighs so much that no one and no two men could carry it off, unless they made several journeys."

"Or there were more of them; they would hardly dare return after one visit."

" Why not ? Hardman (for I know he is at
the bottom of the business) and the other rogue
have been watching us for several days. They
knew that when we left here in the morning
we would not come back till night, and they
had all the time they needed and much more."

" But if there were only two, they would
have to keep doubling their journey, and I
don't believe they would do that. Perhaps
they used the donkey."

" Let's find out."

The burro was accustomed to graze over an
area several acres in extent and enclosed by
walls of rocks. Since the first-mentioned brook
ran alongside, the indolent creature could be
counted upon to remain where the pasture was
succulent and abundant. The place was not
far off, and the boys hurried thither.

A few minutes later the suggestive fact became apparent—the donkey was gone.

" And he helped take the gold !" was the exclamation of Frank. " They loaded part of it
on his back and carried the rest. I don't believe
they are far off."

It was certain the thieves had not gone in
the direction of the diggings, and it was im-

probable that they would attempt to reach Dawson City, at least, for an indefinite time, for they must have known that Jeff Graham and Tim McCabe had gone thither, and that there they were likely to be seen and recognized. At any rate, it would be hard for them to get away through the town for a considerable period, during which the grim old miner would make things warm for them.

The conclusion of the boys, therefore, after briefly debating the problem, was that the men had turned into the mountains. These stretched away for many miles, and contained hundreds of places where they would be safe from pursuit by a regiment of men.

" But if they took the burro," said Roswell, " as it seems certain they did, they must have followed some kind of a path along which we can pursue them."

" Provided we can find it."

They were too much stirred to remain idle. Frank led the way to the corner of the enclosure which was bisected by the brook. There the moistened ground was so spongy that it would disclose any footprint. The marks made by the hoofs of the burro were everywhere, and

THE TELL-TALE FOOTPRINTS.

while examining what seemed to be the freshest, Roswell uttered an exclamation.

" What is it ? " asked his cousin, hurrying to his side.

" Do you see that ? " asked the other in turn, pointing to the ground.

There were the distinct impressions of a pair of heavy shoes. The burro had been loaded at the brook, or his new masters had allowed him to drink before starting into the mountains.

The boys took several minutes to study the impressions, which appeared in a number of places. The inspection brought an interesting truth to light. One set of imprints was large, and the right shoe or boot had a broken patch on the sole, which showed when the ground was more yielding than usual. The others were noticeably smaller, and the toes pointed almost straight forward, like those of an American Indian. A minute examination of the soil failed to bring any other peculiarity to light. The conclusion, therefore, was that only two men were concerned in the robbery.

The problem now assumed a phase which demanded brain work, and the youths met it with a skill that did them credit. The question was :

" If the burro was loaded with the gold at this point, or if he was brought hither, which amounts to the same thing, where did he and the thieves leave the enclosure ? "

Neither of the boys had ever felt enough interest in the animal to make an inspection of his pasturage ground, and therefore knew nothing about it, but scrutinizing the boundaries, they fixed upon two gaps or openings on the farther side, both leading deeper into the mountains, one of which they believed had been used.

" Let's try the nearest," said Roswell, leading the way across the comparatively level space.

There the ground was higher, fairly dry and gravelly. A close scrutiny failed to reveal any signs of disturbance, and forced them to conclude that some other outlet had been taken. They made haste to the second.

This was drier and more gravelly than the other. While the soil seemed to have been disturbed, they could not make sure whether or not it was by the hoofs of an animal, but Frank caught sight of something on a projecting point of a rock, just in front. Stepping forward, he plucked it off, and held it up in the light. It consisted of a dozen dark, coarse hairs.

" That's where the burro scraped against the rock," he said. " We are on their path."

In their eagerness they would have kept beside each other had not the passage been so narrow. Often they came to places where one would have declared it impossible for a mule or donkey to make his way, but there could be no question that the property of Jeff Graham had done it. Frequently he slipped, and must have come near falling, but he managed to keep forward with his precious load.

Less than two hundred yards distant the pursuers came to a depression of the soil where it was damp, and the footprints of the donkey and the two men were as distinct as if made in putty. There could be no question that the boys were on the trail of the despoilers.

As they advanced, Frank, who was in advance, frequently turned his head and spoke in guarded tones over his shoulder to his cousin.

" They are pushing into the mountains," said he, " but there's no saying how far they are ahead of us."

"No; if they made the start early in the morning, it would give them a big advantage."

"I believe that is what they did, knowing there was no danger of our returning until night."

"That knowledge may have made them slow. Anyhow, they are not travelling as fast as we, and we must overtake them before long."

A few minutes later Frank asked:

"Do you believe they have thought of being followed?"

"They must know there is danger of it. They will fight to keep that gold, and if they get the first sight of us will shoot."

"They may have revolvers, but I don't believe either has a rifle. We will keep a lookout that we don't run into them before we know it and give them the advantage."

This dread handicapped the boys to some extent. The trail was not distinctly marked, often winding and precipitous, and compelling them to halt and examine the ground and consult as to their course.

While thus engaged, they awoke to the fact that they had gone astray and were not following the trail at all.

CHAPTER XX.

The error occurred in this way : The trail that the boys had been assiduously following was so faintly marked that the wonder was they did not go astray sooner. In many places, there was little choice as to the route, because it was so broken and crossed that one was as distinct as the other. Nevertheless, Frank pressed on with scarcely any hesitation, until he again reached a depression where the soft ground failed to show the slightest impression of shoe or hoof.

" My gracious !" he exclaimed, stopping short and looking at his companion ; " how far can we have gone wrong ?"

" We can find out only by returning," replied Roswell, wheeling about and leading the way back.

They walked more hurriedly than before, as

a person naturally does who feels that time is precious, and he has wasted a good deal of it.

The search might have been continued for a long time but for a surprising and unexpected aid that came to them. They had halted at one of the broken places, in doubt whither to turn, and searching for some sign to guide them, when Roswell called out :

" That beats anything I ever saw !"

As he spoke, he stooped and picked up something from the ground. Inspecting it for a moment, he held it up for Frank to see. It was a large nugget of pure gold.

" These mountains must be full of the metal," said Frank, " when we find it lying loose like that."

" Not so fast," remarked his companion, who had taken the nugget again, and was turning it over and examining it minutely. " Do you remember that ?"

On one of the faces of the gold something had been scratched with the point of a knife. While the work was inartistic, it was easy to make out the letters " F. M."

" I think I remember that," said Frank ;

" it is one of the nuggets I found yesterday, and marked it with my initials. Those folks must have dropped it."

There could be no doubt of it. What amazing carelessness for a couple of men to drop a chunk of gold worth several hundred dollars and not miss it !

It must have been that the mouth of the canvas bag containing the nuggets had become opened in some way to the extent of allowing a single one to fall out.

" I wonder how many more have been lost," mused Frank, as he put the specimen in his pocket.

At any rate, it served to show the right course to follow, and the boys pressed on, looking more for nuggets than for their enemies. The mishap must have been discovered by the men in time to prevent its repetition, for nothing of the kind again met the eyes of the youths, who once more gave their attention to hunting for the lawless men that had despoiled them of so much property.

The trail steadily ascended, so broken and rough that it was a source of constant wonderment how the burro was able to keep his feet.

He must have had some experience in mountain climbing before, in order to play the chamois so well.

The boys fancied they could feel the change of temperature on account of the increased elevation. They knew they were a good many feet above the starting-point, though at no time were they able to obtain a satisfactory view of the country they were leaving behind. They seemed to be continually passing in and out among the rocks and bowlders, which circumscribed their field of vision. Considerable pine and hemlock grew on all sides, but as yet they encountered no snow. There was plenty of it farther up and beyond, and it would not take them long to reach the region where eternal winter reigned.

A short way along the new course, and they paused before another break; but although the ground was dry and hard, it was easy to follow the course of the burro, whose hoofs told the story; and though nothing served to indicate that the men were still with him, the fact of the three being in company might be set down as self-evident.

It would not be dark until nearly 10 o'clock,

so the pursuers still had a goodly number of hours before them.

A peculiar fact annoyed the boys more than would be supposed. The trail was continually winding in and out, its turns so numerous that rarely or never were they able to see more than a few rods in advance. In places the winding was incessant. The uncertainty as to how far they were behind the donkey and the men made the lads fear that at each turn as they approached it, they would come upon the party, who, perhaps, might be expecting them, and would thus take them unprepared. The dread of something like this often checked the boys and seriously retarded their progress.

"We may as well understand one thing," said Frank, as they halted again; "you have heard Jeff tell about getting the drop on a man, Roswell?"

"Yes; everybody knows what that means."

"Well, neither Mr. Hardman, nor his friend, nor both of them will ever get the drop on us."

The flashing eyes and determined expression left no doubt of the lad's earnestness.

"Is that because you carry a Winchester and they have only their revolvers?"

" It would make no difference if both of them had rifles."

Roswell was thoughtful.

" It is very well, Frank, to be brave, but there's nothing gained by butting your head against a stone wall. Suppose, now, that, in passing the next bend in this path, you should see Hardman waiting for you with his gun aimed, and he should call out to you to surrender, what would you do ?"

" Let fly at him as quickly as I could raise my gun to a level."

" And he would shoot before you could do that."

" I'll take the chances," was the rash response.

" I hope you will not have to take any chances like that—"

They were talking as usual in low tones, and no one more than a few feet away could have caught the murmur of their voices, but while Roswell was uttering his words, and before he could complete his sentence, the two heard a sound, so faint that neither could guess its nature.

As nearly as they were able to judge, it was

WATCHING AT THE TURN IN THE TRAIL.

as if some person, in walking, had struck his foot against an obstruction. It came from a point in front, and apparently just beyond the first bend in the trail, over which they were making their way.

"We are nearer to them than we suspected," whispered Roswell.

"And they don't know it, or they wouldn't have betrayed themselves in that manner."

"It isn't safe to take that for granted."

Roswell, after the last change in their course, was at the front. Frank now quietly moved beyond him, Winchester in hand, and ready for whatever might come. Confident they were close upon the men they sought, he was glad of the misstep that had warned them of the fact.

There certainly could be no excuse now for Hardman and his companion securing the advantage over the boys, when one of them held his Winchester half raised to his shoulder and ready to fire.

Within a couple of paces of the turn in the trail the two were almost lifted off their feet by a sound that burst from the stillness, startling enough to frighten the strongest man. It was the braying of the burro, not fifty feet distant.

CHAPTER XXI

THE boys were in no doubt as to the author of this startling break in the mountain stillness. It was their own burro that had given out the unearthly roar, and they were confident of being close upon the trail of the two men who were making off with the gold. But a moment later, round the corner in front of them, the donkey's head came into view, his long ears flapping, as if training themselves for the fight with mosquitoes that would soon come. The animal was walking slowly, but the astonishing fact immediately appeared that he was not only without any load on his back, but was unaccompanied by either Hardman or his confederate.

Suspecting, however, they were close behind him, the boys held their places, the foremost still on the alert for the criminals. The burro came forward until within a rod, when he seemed to become aware for the first time of the presence of the youths in his path. He halted, twiddled his rabbit-like ears, looked at the two, and then opened his mouth. The flexible lips fluttered and vibrated with a second tremendous bray, which rolled back and forth among the mountains, the wheezing addendum more penetrating than the first part of the outburst.

As the animal showed a disposition to continue his advance, the boys stepped aside and he came slowly forward, as if in doubt whether he was doing a prudent thing ; but he kept on, and, passing both, continued down the trail, evidently anxious to return to his pasturage.

" What does it mean ?" asked Roswell.

" I have no idea, unless—"

" What ?"

" They can't make any further use of the burro, and have allowed him to go home."

" But they can't carry away all the gold."

" Then they are burying it. Let's hurry on, or we shall be too late."

Lowering his Winchester, Frank led the way up the trail, slackening his pace as he reached the bend, and partly raising his weapon again.

Rocks and bowlders were all around, but the trail still showed, and the donkey could have travelled indefinitely forward, so far as the boys could see. Nowhere was anything detected of the two men.

"They may have turned the burro loose a half mile off," said Frank, chagrined and disappointed beyond expression.

His companion warned him to be careful, as he began pushing forward at a reckless rate, as if fearful that the men would get away after all.

Just beyond the point where the burro had appeared the path forked, each course being equally distinct. The boys scrutinized the ground, but could not decide from what direction the animal had come. Had they possessed the patience, they might have settled the question by kneeling down and making their scrutiny more minute; but Frank could not wait.

"I'll take the right," he said, "while you follow the left. If you discover either of them, shoot and shout for me."

It may be doubted whether this was wise counsel, and Roswell did not feel himself bound by it, but he acted at once upon the suggestion. His weapon was in his grasp as he hurried over the path, and the cousins were quickly lost to each other.

The inspiring incentive to both boys was the dread that they were too late to recover the gold that had been stolen. Since its weight was too great for a couple of men to carry, the natural presumption was that they had buried or would bury it in some secure place, and return when it was safe to take it away.

Because of this, Roswell Palmer sharply scrutinized every part of his field of vision as it opened before him. There were numerous breaks in the path which permitted him to look over a space of several rods, and again he could not see six feet from him.

Reaching an earthy part of the trail, he leaned over and studied it. There was no sign of a hoof or footprint.

"The burro did not come this far," was his conclusion; "I am wasting time by wandering from Frank."

He was in doubt whether to turn or to advance farther. He had paused among the bowlders, where little was visible, and, convinced of his mistake, he shoved his weapon back in his pocket, so as to give him the freer use of his hands, and turned back over the trail along which he had just come.

He had not taken a dozen steps when he was checked by the most startling summons that could come to him. It was a gruff " Hands up, younker !"

It will be recalled that Roswell was less headstrong than his cousin, as he now demonstrated by his prompt obedience to the command, which came from an immense rock at the side of the path, partly behind him.

Having elevated his hands, the youth turned to look at his master. One glance at the countenance was sufficient. He was the individual whom Frank had seen secretly talking with Hardman on the boat that carried them from the head to the foot of Lake Lindeman, and whom both had seen on the day of their arrival in this neighborhood.

Roswell Palmer now displayed a quickness of wit that would have done credit to an older head. His revolver he had placed in a pocket on the side of him that was turned away from the man, and it will be remembered that the lad had placed it there before receiving the peremptory summons to surrender. In the

"HANDS UP, YOUNKER!"

hope that his captor was not aware that he carried any firearms, Roswell kept that part of his body farthest from him.

The man was standing at the side of the rock with a similar weapon in his grasp, and showed that he was elated over the clever manner in which he had gotten the best of the youth. His own weapon was not pointed at him, but held so that it could be raised and used on the instant.

"What do you mean by treating me thus when I am walking peaceably through the mountains, offering harm to no one?" asked Roswell with an injured air.

"What are you doing here anyway?" demanded the other, whose unpleasant face indicated that he did not fully grasp the situation.

"My friend and I set out to look for some men that have stolen our gold. Have you seen them?"

This sounded as if the boy had no suspicion of the fellow before him, and taking his cue therefrom, he said:

"No; I don't know anything about it. Did they jump your claim?"

"We had the gold among the rocks where

we live, but when we came home to-day, we found that some persons had been there and taken it all."

Something seemed to strike the man as very amusing. He broke into laughter.

" You can put down your hands, my son, if you're getting tired."

" You won't shoot?" asked Roswell in pretended alarm.

" Not much," replied the other, with a laugh ; " I haven't a charge in my weapon nor a single cartridge with me; but all the same, I'll keep an eye on you."

" Not doubting your word, I have to inform you that my pistol is loaded, and I now shall take charge of you."

As he spoke, Roswell produced his weapon, and the other was at his mercy.

CHAPTER XXII.

A LION IN THE PATH.

To put it mildly, the man was astonished. Not dreaming the boy was armed, he had been foolish enough to announce that he had brought him to terms by the display of a useless weapon. He stared in amazement at Roswell, and then elevated both hands. The boy laughed.

" You needn't do that ; I am not afraid of you. If you will lead me to the spot where you and Hardman hid our gold, I will set you free."

" I don't know anything about your gold," whimpered the fellow, who now proved himself a coward. " I was only joking with you."

" You and he took it. I shall hold you a prisoner until my friend comes up, and then turn you over to the mounted police."

" All right ; if it is a square deal, follow me."

He turned and darted behind the rock. The

youth made after him, but when he came in sight of the fugitive again he was fifty feet distant, and running like a deer. Perhaps Roswell might have winged him, but he did not try to do so. He felt a natural repugnance to doing a thing of that nature, and the fact was self-evident that it would do no good. The man would sturdily insist that he knew nothing of the missing gold, and there could be no actual proof that he did. Had he been held a prisoner he might have been forced to terms, but it was too late now to think of that, and the youth stood motionless and saw him disappear among the rocks.

"I wonder how Frank has made out," was his thought. "He can't have done worse than I."

Meanwhile, young Mansley had no idle time on his hands. He had hurried up the fork of the trail, after parting with his companion, until he had passed about the same distance. The two paths, although diverging, did not do so to the extent the boys thought, and thus it came about that they were considerably nearer each other than they supposed.

It need not be said that Frank was on the

alert. Suspecting he was in the vicinity of the men for whom they were searching, he paid no attention to the ground, but glanced keenly to the right and left, and even behind him. He was thus engaged when something moved beside a craggy mass of rocks a little way ahead and slightly to the right of the path he was following. A second look showed the object to be a man, and though his back was toward the lad, his dress and general appearance left little doubt that he was Hardman.

His attitude was that of listening. His shoulders were thrown slightly forward, and he gave a quick flirt of his head, which brought his profile for the moment into view. This removed all doubt as to his identity. It was Ike Hardman.

Frank's first thought was that he was standing near the spot where the gold had been secreted, and was looking around to make sure no one saw him, but it may have been he heard something of the movements of his confederate that had escaped Roswell Palmer.

Afraid of being detected, Frank crouched behind the nearest bowlder, but was a second too late. Hardman had observed him, and was off like a flash. To Frank's amazement, when he looked for him he was gone.

Determined not to lose him, the youth ran forward as fast as the nature of the ground would permit. Reaching the spot where he had first discovered the man, he glanced at the surroundings, but could see nothing to indicate that the gold had been hidden anywhere near, though the probabilities pointed to such being the fact, for it must have been in that vicinity that the burro was turned free.

But the boy felt the necessity of bringing the man himself to terms, and with scarcely a halt he hurried over the bowlders and around the rocks in what he believed to be the right direction, though he had no certain knowledge that such was the fact.

He was still clambering forward, panting, impatient, and angry, when a figure suddenly came to view a little way in advance. Frank abruptly stopped and brought his gun to a level, but before he could aim he perceived to his amazement that it was his cousin Roswell standing motionless and looking with wonderment around him. A moment later the two came together and hastily exchanged experiences.

"WE HAVE MADE A MESS OF IT," WAS THE DISGUSTED
COMMENT OF FRANK.

" We have made a mess of it," was the disgusted comment of Frank, " for we had them both and let them get away."

" All the same we must be near the spot where the gold was hidden, and I believe we can find it by searching."

" We may, but the chances are a hundred to one against it. How strange that those two men carried no firearms !"

It has been shown that the Klondike country is not one of dangerous weapons, because it is well governed, and the necessity, therefore, does not exist for men to go about armed. Many of them unquestionably carry pistols, but larger weapons are few, and the majority have neither, for they only serve as incumbrances. Strange, therefore, as it may seem, Hardman and his companion had but a single revolver between them, and the man who carried that spoke the truth when he said all its chambers were empty and he was without the means of loading it.

The great oversight of the two was that when they entered the cavern and took away the gold, they left the Winchester and revolvers. This may have been due to their eagerness to carry off every ounce of gold, but the commonest prudence would have suggested that they " spike" the weapons, so as to prevent their being used against them.

A brief consultation caused the boys to decide to return to the cavern and await the return of their friends. Then the whole party could take up the search, though it seemed almost hopeless.

Disheartened, they started down the trail, Frank in advance and both silent, for their thoughts were too depressing for expression. Suddenly the leader stopped and raised his hand for his companion to do the same. The cause was apparent, for at that moment, in rounding a bend in the path, they saw Ike Hardman in front, moving stealthily in the same direction with themselves, but the rogue was watchful and caught sight of them at the same moment. As before, he was off like an arrow, the winding trail allowing him to pass from sight in the twinkling of an eye, as may be said.

Before they could take up the pursuit a great commotion broke out below them, and wondering what it could mean, the boys stopped to listen. It immediately became apparent that

the fugitive had come in collision with some
one approaching from the other direction over
the trail, and that same person was gifted
with a vigorous voice of which he was making
free use.

" Ah, but ye are the spalpeen I've been looking fur! This is the way ye sittle up fur the
money ye tuk from me! Mister Hardman, do
your bist, for that's what I'm going to do. Do
ye hear me?"

" It's Tim!" exclaimed Roswell: " let's
hurry to his help!"

But Frank caught his arm.

" It's the other fellow who needs help, and
Tim will take it as unkind for us to interfere,
but we can look on."

And they hurried forward.

CHAPTER XXIII.

A GENERAL SETTLEMENT OF ACCOUNTS.

QUICK as were the boys in hurrying to the point where they heard the indignant Tim, they did not reach it until the affray was over. Wholly subdued, Ike Hardman begged for mercy at the hands of his conqueror, and promised to do anything desired if he received consideration.

It is a well-known fact that the wrath of a good-natured person is more to be feared than his who is of less equable temperament. The boys had never seen Tim McCabe in so dangerous a mood. He and Jeff Graham had returned to the cavern shortly after the departure of the cousins in pursuit of the thieves, and it did not take them long to understand what had occurred. They set out over the same trail, along which they readily discovered the footprints of all the parties. Tim, in his angry impatience, outsped his more stolid companion, and by good fortune came upon Hardman while in headlong flight down the mountain path.

The latter tried for a time to make it appear that he knew nothing of the abstraction of the gold from the cavern, but Tim would have none of it, and gave him the choice of conducting them to the place where it was concealed or of undergoing " capital punishment." Like the poltroon that he was, Hardman insisted that his companion, Victor Herzog, was the real wrongdoer, but he offered to do what was demanded, only imploring that he should not be harmed for his evil acts.

Tim extended his hand and took the Winchester from Frank Mansley. He knew it was loaded, and he said to his prisoner :

" Lead on, and if ye think it will pay ye to try to git away or play any of yer tricks, why try it, that's all !''

The threat was sufficient to banish all hope from Hardman, who led them along the trail a short way, then turned on to the pile of rocks beside which Frank had seen him standing a short time before.

" There it is !" he said, with an apprehensive glance at his captor.

" Where ?" thundered Tim ; " I don't see it !"

No digging had been done by the criminals, but a bowlder had been rolled aside, the canvas bags dropped into the opening, and the stone replaced, as he quickly demonstrated.

" Count 'em, Roswell," said Tim.

Both boys leaned over, and moving the heavy sacks about so as not to miss one, announced that all were there.

" And now I s'pose I may go," whined Hardman.

" Not a bit of it. I won't make a target of ye fer this gun, but ye shall remain me prisoner till I turn ye over to the police."

Thereupon Hardman begged so piteously that the boys interceded and asked that he be allowed to go, but Tim sternly bade them hold their peace. The bowlder having been replaced, while he glanced around to fix the locality in his memory, he ordered the captive to precede him down the trail, reminding him at the same time that the first attempt on his part to escape would be followed by the instant discharge of the gun.

Thus, as the long afternoon drew to a close

the strange procession wound its way down the mountain, the prisoner in front, his captors directly behind, with Frank and Roswell bringing up the rear. The boys talked in whispers, but said nothing to their friend, who was in such a stern mood that they shrank from speaking to him.

They speculated as to the fate of Herzog, the other criminal, who seemed to have effected his escape, but recalled that Jeff Graham was likely to be met somewhere along the path, and it might be that this had occurred with disastrous results to the evil fellow, for it will be remembered that the old miner was one of the few who always carried their revolvers with them.

The expectation of the boys was not disappointed. When about half way down the trail they came upon Jeff, who had his man secure, thanks to the good fortune which gave him an advantage of which he instantly availed himself.

Roswell and Frank thought that when Jeff learned that all the stolen gold had been recovered he would be willing to release the prisoners, but such intention was as far from him as from Tim McCabe. While he had no desire for revenge, he felt it would be wrong to set the evil-doers free, and he knew that they would receive the punishment they had well earned as soon as placed within the power of the law.

It was beginning to grow dark when the party reached their cabin. Just before reaching it they crossed the pasturage ground of the burro, who was seen quietly browsing, as if he had not taken any part and felt no interest in the proceedings of the afternoon.

Halting in front of the opening, Jeff said to Tim :

" You have the gun and know it's a re-peater."

The Irishman nodded his head.

" Keep guard over these fellows till I come back; it won't be long."

" I'll do the same—on that ye may depind."

The massive figure swung off in the gloom. He gave no intimation of whither he was going, and no one could guess, except that he promised shortly to return.

A few minutes after his departure, both Hard-man and Herzog renewed their pleadings for mercy—for at least they suspected the cause of

TIM AND HIS PRISONERS.

the old miner's departure—but Tim checked them so promptly that they held their peace.

At his suggestion, the boys started a fire and began preparing supper. They had hardly completed the task when Jeff Graham reappeared and he brought two companions with him. Though they were on foot, they were members of the mounted police, whose horses were but a short distance away. In the discharge of their duties, they were on a tour among the diggings to learn whether there was any call for their services. Jeff had seen them during the afternoon, and knew where to look for them.

There was no nonsense about those sturdy fellows. They made their living by compelling obedience to the laws of their country, and were always prepared to do their duty. At the suggestion of Jeff, they questioned the men, who admitted their guilt, supplementing the confession with another appeal for clemency. Without deigning a reply, the officers slipped handcuffs upon them, and declining the invitation to remain to supper, departed with their prisoners, whom they delivered to the authorities at Dawson City on the following day.

Since they had admitted their guilt, our friends were not required to appear as witnesses, and the case may be closed by the statement that Hardman and Herzog received the full punishment which they deserved.

When the evening meal was finished, the men and boys remained outside in the cool, clear air, the former smoking their pipes, and all discussing the stirring events of the day. The boys confessed their neglect in failing to make known the presence of Herzog in the neighborhood, because the fact was driven from their minds by their excitement over the discovery of gold.

" Had we done as we ought," said Frank, " it isn't likely this would have happened."

" You are right," replied Jeff, " for we should have been more watchful."

" And wasn't it oursilves that was careless, anyway, in laying so much wilth where any one could git at the same ?" asked Tim.

" Yes," admitted the old miner, " but things are different here from what they was in the early days in Californy, and you can see that these two men are the only ones that would steal our stuff."

" At prisint they saam to be the only ones, but we can't be sure that ithers wouldn't have tried to do the same."

" Well, boys," was the surprising announcement of Jeff Graham, " to-morrow we leave this place for good and take the next steamer down the Yukon for home ; our hunt for gold is done '"

CHAPTER XXIV.

CONCLUSION.

THERE was little sleep that night in the cavern home of the gold-seekers. The fact that the whole crop of the precious stuff was the better part of a mile away in the mountains, even though apparently safe, caused every one to feel uneasy. In addition was the announcement of Jeff Graham, the leader, that their work in the Klondike region was ended. In keeping with his habit of making known only that which was necessary, he gave no explanation, and his friends were left to speculate and surmise among themselves. All, however, suspected the truth.

At early dawn Tim McCabe and the boys started up the trail, leading the burro. The old miner remained behind, saying that he expected company and his help was not needed in recovering the pilfered gold. The anxiety of the men and boys did not lessen until they reached the well-remembered spot and found the canvas bags intact. They were carefully loaded upon the strong back of the animal, secured in place, and the homeward journey begun. Frank and Roswell walked at the rear, to make sure none of the gold was lost. In due time they reached their primitive home, with all their wealth in hand.

To their surprise, Jeff was absent. The recent experience of the three confirmed them in their resolution not to leave the nuggets and dust unguarded for a single hour. While some were at work in the diggings, one at least would be at the cavern on the watch against dishonest visitors. It was agreed that Tim and Roswell should go to the little valley to resume work, while Frank with the Winchester and smaller weapon acted as sentinel.

As the two were on the point of setting out, Jeff Graham appeared with two well-dressed gentlemen, both in middle life. They were talking earnestly, and halted just beyond ear-shot to complete what they had to say. Then, without waiting to be introduced to Jeff's friends, they bade him good-day, and hurried down the path to where their horses were waiting, and lost no time in returning to Dawson City.

"Get ready to foller," was the curt command of Jeff; and within the following hour the whole party, including the donkey, were on the road. They were compelled to spend one of the short nights in camp, but reached Dawson City without the slightest molestation from any one or the loss of a dollar's worth of gold. As Jeff had announced his intention, they brought away only their auriferous harvest and such clothing as was on their bodies. At the hotel he held another long interview with the two gentlemen who had called on him at the diggings; and the first steamer down the Yukon, which was now fairly open, bore among its hundreds of passengers Jeff Graham, Tim McCabe, Roswell Palmer, and Frank Mansley. The combined gold of the fortunate passengers on that trip must have amounted to nearly a million dollars.

Some weeks later Jeff and Tim were seated alone in one of the rooms at the Palace Hotel, San Francisco. They had met by appointment to close up the business which had taken them into the Klondike region.

" You know, Tim," said the old miner, " that this whole thing was my own."

Tim nodded his head.

" I was aware of the same before ye mentioned it. Ye paid all our ixpenses like a gintleman, and we're entitled to fair wages for hilping and no more."

The generous disavowal of all claim to a share in the rich find touched Jeff, who hastened to say :

" Some folks might think that way, but I don't. It was a speculation on my part. It didn't cost much to get us to the Klondike, and so that don't count. I have delivered to the mint all the gold we brought back, and have been paid one hundred and twenty thousand dollars for it. You know what was done by the two men that visited us at the diggings ?"

" The byes and mesilf had the idea that they bought out your claim."

" That's it. I was anxious to get out of the country before the summer fairly set in and the mosquitoes ate us up alive. From the way the dirt panned out, we should have been millionaires in a few weeks, but we had enough. There ain't many men as know when they have

enough," was the philosophical observation of
Jeff. " I do, so I sold my claim for a hundred
and eighty thousand dollars. As I figure out,
that makes the total three hundred thousand
dollars, which, divided among us four, gives
each seventy-five thousand dollars. How does
that strike you, Tim ?"

" It almost knocks me off my chair, if you
mean it."

" The boys being under age, I have turned
over their shares to their parents ; and do you
know," added Jeff, with an expression of disgust, " they both fixed things so as to go to
college ? You wouldn't believe it, but it's the
fact. Howsumever, it's their business, and I
ain't saying anything. Say, Tim, you hain't
any idea of going to college ?" asked Jeff,
looking across at his friend with a startled expression.

" I won't unless ye will go wid me. How
does that strike ye ?"

Jeff's shoulders bobbed up and down with
silent laughter, and immediately he became
serious again.

" As soon as you sign this paper, Tim, I shall
give you a certified check for seventy-five thou-

"SAY, TIM, YOU HAIN'T ANY IDEA OF GOING TO COLLEGE, HAVE YOU?"

sand dollars on the Bank of Californy. Are you ready to sign?"

"I'll sign me own death warrant for that trifle," replied Tim, his rosy face aglow, as he caught up the pen.

"Read it first."

His friend read :

"I, Timothy McCabe, hereby pledge my sacred honor not to taste a drop of malt or spirituous liquor, even on the advice of a physician who may declare it necessary to save my life, from the date of the signing of this pledge until the Fourth of July, one thousand nine hundred and seven."

As Tim gathered the meaning of the words on the paper, his eyes expanded ; he puckered his lips and emitted a low whistle.

"Do ye mind," he said, looking across the table with his old quizzical expression, "the remark that the governor of North Carliny made to the governor of South Carliny ?"

Jeff gravely inclined his head.

"I've heerd of it."

"What do ye s'pose he would have said if the time between drinks was ten years ?"

"I've never thought, and don't care."

"He would have died long before the time was up."

"When you left the boys in the diggings you came to Dawson City to spend the worth of that nugget for whiskey. I happened to meet you in time and made you go back with me. You'd been off on sprees a half dozen other times, if I hadn't kept an eye on you. Drink is the enemy that will down you if you don't stop at once. If you'll stay sober for ten years, I'll take the chances after that. Are you going to sign?"

Tim's eyes were fixed on the paper which he held in his hand. He mused loud enough for the listening Jeff to catch every word:

"To sign that means no more headaches and bad health, but a clear brain and a strong body; no more hours of gloom, no weakness of the limbs and pricks of the conscience; no more breaking the heart of me good old mother in Ireland, but the bringing of sunshine and joy to her in her last days; it means the signing away of me slavery, and the clasping to me heart of the swate boon of liberty; it means the making of mesilf into a man!"

With a firm hand he wrote his name at the

bottom of the paper, and flinging down the pen, said :

" With God's help, that pledge shall be kept. "

" Amen," reverently responded Jeff; " there's your check for seventy-five thousand dollars. "

THE END.

www.ingramcontent.com/pod-product-compliance
Lightning Source LLC
Chambersburg PA
CBHW030642030726
47497CB00006B/1916